PICK UP STICK CITY

Steven H Semken

River's Bend Press
Stillwater, Minnesota

Pick Up Stick City

Copyright © 2005 Steven H. Semken

First Edition

ISBN 0-9729445-1-6

Published by River's Bend Press
Post Office Box 606
Stillwater, Minnesota 55082 USA
www.riversbendpress.com

The paper used in this publication meets the mini-
mum requirements of the American National Standard for Information Sciences—Permanence of Paper
for Printed Library Materials, ANSI Z39.48-1992

Cover design © Stefan Knorr
www.stefanknorrdesign.com

Library of Congress Cataloging-in-Publication Data

Semken, S. H. (Steven H.)
  Pick up stick city / by Steven H. Semken.— 1st ed.
     p. cm.
  ISBN 0-9729445-1-6 (alk. paper)
  1. Ghost towns—Fiction. 2. Drifters—Fiction. I.
Title.

  PS3569.E587P53 2005
  813'.54--dc22
                      2005016889

ACKNOWLEDGEMENTS

Really 'n truly I worked on, revised, added, took away and considered throwing away this book in at least eight different states that I can remember—Kansas, Michigan, Missouri, Oregon, California, Wisconsin, Alaska and Iowa—over the course of eight years. The length has ranged anywhere from fifty pages to well over two hundred and fifty. Along the way I learned a lot of things, the most "novel" lesson being that if you make a change on page 14, this means changes must be made on pages 16, 17, 18, 45, 78, 90, 113, 211, and so on! Thanks to Laura "my funny valentine" and a wave of funky music to Fenna Marie "the greatest kid." Once upon a time, on a dark and stormy morning in a galaxy now seemingly far away in 1994, I was standing along a trout stream in Missouri with a friend of mine and I said, "I'll be happy if I can get a small novel published by the time I'm forty!" Perhaps the world was paying attention. I received news from River's Bend Press, literally, when I was thirty-nine years, three hundred and sixty-two days old...whew, that was a close one. Take my word for it, the world would be a scary place if it weren't for brilliant editors and committed book publishers. I offer a bow of praise and many wonderful thanks to Jane Esbensen for spotting *Pick Up Stick City* from amongst the many submissions she is sent. Additionally, her work as an editor has been nothing short of genius. Having the skill to form a concise story out of the mish-mashed, emotionally threaded scenarios I placed before her was no small task. Gratitudes to William Schmaltz, too. His "letter of acceptance" ranks as one of the most enjoyable pieces of writing I've ever read. In the end, any work of creativity requires the help of many and I am lucky to have had many.

NOTE:

THIS STORY IS NOT A CONFESSION, NOR AM I IN TROUBLE WITH THE LAW, YET PERHAPS YOU'D PREFER TO HEAR THIS STRAIGHT OFF SINCE LATER ON THIS CHRONICLE OF LIFE MAY REQUIRE THAT YOU FEEL SECURE AND IN NEED OF A CERTAIN GUARANTEE OF HONESTY. THEREFORE—LET IT BE KNOWN THAT WHAT YOU ARE ABOUT TO READ IS THE WHOLE TRUTH AND NOTHING BUT THE TRUTH SO HELP ME GOD & FROM THE PIT OF MY HONEST HEART I PROMISE NO ATTEMPTS MADE IN ORDER TO LEAD THE READER ASTRAY FROM THAT WHICH HAS TRULY HAPPENED—H. TRENCHOLD

PREAMBLE

Standing amidst the ruins of a ghost town, Harness paused a moment. There were noises in the wind. Putting his ear alongside an old windowpane, he held his breath and listened. In the background there were noises, light scrapings, gentle tappings, whispers—voices from the past. The land and the ruins, all the spirits and mysteries seemed anxious to release hearsay and legends, stories and dreams.

As he had longed to do since he had played with imaginary friends in the woods behind his house as a little child, Harness Trenchold had become involved in a miracle, deep in a hilly and abandoned portion of Iowa, where rusty barbed wire and small family farms still clung to the memories of the older residents. All of his senses, hopes and dreams started working together as he discovered a fascinating collage of the past amongst the ruins of a small ghost town the year he turned thirty-two.

Harness' adventures occurred apart from big cities and popular commercials: it's possible to imagine that his reality had been too narrow, too innocent, of no consequence. However, it will become clear: his reality had been far-reaching.

* * * * *

When the posted arrival time for the freight train was moved back another two hours, Harness Trenchold surprised no one when he looked around with his gap-toothed grin, raised his arms up high, clenched his hands into fists, arched his back and stuttered a stream of grunts like he was chewing gravel. After this torrent of noise, he looked to the ground and drew his lips tightly together before cracking up in a short, two-second giggle. He then flipped his head side to side, popping his tense and rigid neck.

For three days now Harness had been waiting in the rain at the Fargas Union train depot. All over and around him persistent pads of water continued to splatter and slosh in deep puddles, the drops plodding and plunking on the earth like heartbeats. Waiting, Harness spent most of the time pacing back and forth, roughly twenty steps. Teamed with the movement of his feet was a stream of anxious thoughts bunched up, racing haphazardly through his mind.

Three days ago he'd been in no condition to wait. Now he was just plain dangerous. He was ready to bicker with a speck of dust. Not social in appearance, or attitude, Harness had become a ragged spectacle. His hair clung together in greasy spikes, his clothing was spotted with dirt, and his breath reeked of thin, raunchy coffee. He wore multiple layers of dark-colored wool and cotton clothing all of which was extensively stained and patched. No one crowded Harness while he waited. No one told him why the train was running late.

Throughout Harness' wait, unbeknownst to himself, he had been muttering random noises under his breath, in tones so awkward no one in Fargas Union would, or could, have possibly understood anything he was hinting at. Maintaining an aura of civilized behavior had long ago stopped being part of Harness' attitude. After all, he'd become accustomed to sharing his life with ghosts.

CHAPTER ONE

Harness Trenchold was a well-known stranger to everyone in the village of Fargas Union. In fact, the sight of him had become enough to scatter most when he approached. He presented people with nothing they could predict or easily understand. This strangeness left others tense, because Harness never tried to hide the fact that he was different. He even had a bumper sticker on his truck that read, "NO ONE IS BORN ALIKE, PROVE IT!"

The general consensus about Harness was that he was simply of an anti-establishment bent or, worse yet, being different just to be different. However, in a rather mock-scientific way, it's worth noting Harness had neither proved nor disproved these beliefs completely.

Although a letdown, most people in Fargas Union had come to agree: there was no crime in just being strange. In fact, although they wouldn't admit it, some of the older people, retired mechanics and newspaper writers for instance, as well as some of the older farmers who had relocated to town, found Harness' eccentric qualities a welcome relief from the modern era's repetitive, somewhat pastel-based thought patterns. Most found modern life a series of patty-cake actions, the ugly being disguised as beautiful. One old man, Stale Whims, commented how he'd laughed when he read in a small Arkansas newspaper about people taking the *ugh* out of doughnut. "It don't make the donut any easier to eat spelling it that a-ways, just makes people think they're not getting the bad parts. But sure as the spring rains they still getting the *ugh*."

While staring up at a drip in the depot roof, Harness at last heard a train whistle. Far away, the belching blast of noise funneled and echoed down into his inner ear. He walked out to the edge of the platform, beside the tracks, to glare out along the narrowing strips of iron. Squinting his eyes, he looked out as far as his ears could hear. The train he'd been waiting for was coming around the final curve.

As the engine came into full view, it let out another huge, muffled yowl, slowing down as gently as heavy iron can, steam and compressed air moving, drifting wildly about. Harness smoothed a slight smirk across his face and pulled in a long breath of steam-filled air. His wait was over.

With eyes peering at him from a safe and silent distance, Harness moved to the freight car and held up six baggage claims for the attendant to see. The attendant took the claim tickets and returned six times, each time with a sturdy-sided container that looked large enough to hold two, maybe three bushels of harvested corn. One by one, Harness carried each parcel to the rear of his truck and placed them down, side by side. The few bystanders watching wanted badly to ask Harness what he had waited so patiently for, but no one did. They were all certain that either Harness wouldn't tell them, or if he had told them, they would have been extremely uncomfortable with his answer.

While the bystanders contemplated what was going on, Harness was experiencing joy. The tension of the previous days' wait had lifted, and he was now filled with a sudden feeling of jumpy, childish glee. Picking up his boxes, he imagined he was a hummingbird, wings beating and buzzing in rapid motion. He was also cheerful about the continued intensity of the rain. He hoped the weather would remain wet and drizzly for many more days. In fact, he was counting on rainy weather for at least another four days.

After he'd loaded all the boxes, Harness shook his wet head, jumped into his truck and drove away. As he sped along, he was sure that he was being carried inches off the ground by what he could only believe were the blissful, honey-filled drippings of angel love. His mind was lightheaded, his hands felt soft, his shoulders seemed connected to the clouds above. He was in a glorious and ecstatic state of mind.

CHAPTER TWO

Harness lived in an old ghost town he'd purchased years ago, the town of Siren Falls, although he called it Pick Up Stick City. The old town had once been home to a sixty-foot waterfall which fell smack dab hard onto an enormous chunk of resonant and allegedly well-tuned granite. The crash of the water made a constant whining, alarming echo. Hence the name Siren Falls.

In its day, the supply of water made the town a perfect location for steam trains to stop. The town's major claim to fame, however, had been a short-lived but successful industry of Midwestern hop growing, the key bittering and flavoring ingredient for both ale and lager beers.

Harness had gathered from newspapers lying about in the corners of the ghost town that the place had gone to pot because of a few years of drought and an increase in soil acidity, which caused the local hops to lose their aromatic qualities. As a result, half the town was relocated out of state to a new hop farm in Oregon. Harness had a hard time believing that the entire town had fallen to pieces entirely because of a drought. After all, there seemed to be clues that a large part of the townsfolk had been opposed to beer and hops, clues he had found in some temperance notebooks he discovered in an attic one day.

Additional speculation relating to the disappearance of the town was that perhaps the river which formed the waterfall became so contaminated from fertilizer run-off that all the water in the area was no longer fit to drink or cultivate crops with. This seemed a bit unlikely to

Harness; he wasn't sure when ammonia nitrate fertilizing began but probably not that long ago. Maybe there had been too many cattle on the surrounding land, which resulted in too much manure flowing into the river water. Whatever the cause, it did seem that the water plants had grown so much that the waterfall ceased to flow, making the once splendid Siren Falls no more than a drip of bad water. When the waterfall went silent, Harness reasoned, it probably took the pride of the people away as well. After all, who would want to live in a place named for something that no longer existed? Harness didn't know for certain what had happened, and he doubted if he ever would know completely.

Looking around the first time, Harness guessed the place had been abandoned close to forty-five or fifty years; people had just packed up and left from the looks of it.

Fargas Union was twenty miles away by road, downstream, and was also nestled along the Siren River. The village supported a fertilizer distribution warehouse, one assembly of a radically conservative branch of Lutheran worshippers, a post office, hardware store, grocery store, gas station, First National Bank outlet (actually the second First National, as the original bank burned down three years after it was built in the early 1900s), a grain co-op with six tall silo bins alongside the railroad tracks, a freight and passenger train depot, as well as a diner that also sold bait and tackle plus tripled as a drugstore. Most of the time you could get whatever you wanted at one of the establishments in town. As many of the town folks were prone to saying about their limited resources, "If you don't know any different, then you aren't missing nothing, are you?"

There were about 375 folks that made up Fargas Union. The town itself served another hundred or so people in the outlying area. Most of the other hundred lived in a trailer home park a few miles outside of Fargas Union.

Most were employed by a meat packing plant thirteen miles north of Fargas Union in Sputter Township, the opposite direction of Pick Up Stick City.

As far as Harness was concerned, Fargas Union was soon to become the outer limit of his world. In fact, since his initial arrival a little over seven years ago, most people who bothered keeping an eye on Harness wondered how such a young-looking man could go so long without traveling. During an active year, Harness might visit Fargas Union once. In the beginning he came to town a little more often, but over the last few years hardly a soul ever saw him. Someone had sent the Lutheran pastor out once to speak with Harness, and the man of the Lord returned somewhat sooner than seemed appropriate. The Pastor declared that "although Harness wasn't a Lutheran, he did not appear to have any shortcomings regarding spiritual matters in his life." As for social appearances, Harness' wait at the train depot was by far the longest stay he'd ever made in public.

It was during the first three or four years, when Harness was developing Pick Up Stick City, that people got their opinions settled. Harness turned out to be the type of character that people knew little about and had no desire to know more. He was the kind of person who would tell you a story revolving around something that seemed to make no sense. He might start talking about the weather forecast, suddenly stop midstream, pause, change the subject to geese, then change subjects again, going on and on about a certain noise he was hearing right then and there, which no one else could hear, all while standing right in front of you. Then, because he seemed to talk about things no one else could make head nor tail of, folks felt even less comfortable asking him to repeat what made no sense in the first place. Out of pity, politeness and maybe a tinge of bitterness, people tried to ignore Harness. In the end, he didn't really seem worth the time to understand.

It hadn't always been like that, however. There had been excitement when he first arrived. A good number of folks in Fargas Union wanted a new story, wanted a new legend for their town. They watched carefully and would have accepted most things. In fact, just about anything less than criminally insane would have been welcome. It wasn't an unfair desire for the folks of Fargas Union, either. People started with the assumption that there would be something to know. After all, it's hard to ignore a stranger completely.

Minds don't settle on the idea of nothing very easily, though. Word got out that Harness was living with his extended family out at Pick Up Stick City, that he was living with aunts, uncles, grandparents, faithful friends, as well as twelve brothers and six sisters. And, as if that wasn't enough, someone added, "not to mention seven holy spirits he's been conversing with."

Some of the less friendly people in town suggested Harness was involved in a type of grotesque inbreeding, but this had no credence and was the result of nerves because, try as people might, no one seemed able to spot anyone but Harness living out at his self-proclaimed Pick Up Stick City.

Chapter Three

Well, rumors began to fly left and right when Rufus Splatter claimed he saw a big trunk of mail show up at the post office for a variety of people with the last name of Trenchold living out at Pick Up Stick City. There was never any certainty to this trunk of mail, though. So it was agreed that if no one actually saw the mail except the oftentimes inventive mind of Rufus Splatter, then it probably didn't happen. As with anything, however, some people wanted to cling to this story and told it to visitors and family members once in awhile. There was something about telling Rufus' story that made people feel clever.

The hope for a good story is strong, a thing people crave. For instance, the rumored trunk of mail that showed up for Harness and his family grew and grew. Before long the story being told was that a large metal trunk of mail had arrived, filled with old letters (some stuffed inside corked bottles), a dozen eggs, as well as eight dozen butterflies that had all come flying out when the trunk was opened. There were also supposedly a few boxes that contained a variety of items such as hubcaps, deer horns, zippers, zebra hides, a baseball bat signed by Babe Ruth and some small, brightly colored paintings of the Virgin Mary.

Proud of his new status as storyteller, Rufus told everyone, "See, like I said, now we've got ourselves a mystery. That place out there ain't a town; it's the fantasy land of that Mr. Tarnished Henchman, the witch doctor!"

Rufus seemed to have a point when people started thinking, how could mail be delivered to a made-up place? Rumbling got going and sneers slowly built into a frenzy. Rufus Splatter kept egging people on for weeks with his tale, until one day, Fargas Union Mayor Hardy Popper called to everyone's attention that only Rufus had claimed to see the delivery in question. When Hardy Popper challenged Rufus to better explain the details, to show everyone the mail, to prove he had really seen the butterflies, the bottles and all the rest of the stuff, Rufus Splatter shook his head and seemed offended that he was being doubted. "Don't believe me? Well, you'll see, it's true; we're all in danger now that that Harness Tarnation fella has picked up his communist orders to take over this part of the world."

The same day Hardy Popper spoke to everyone, Mack Stems, who ran the post office, had joined with Hardy Popper to help dispel the rants of Rufus. Mack told people that if any such mail had been delivered, he'd have seen it. He was amazed at all the hype. "No one's believed in ghosts around here as long as I can remember, so it seems a bit strange everyone would start doing so now. Plus, it's just not fair for any of us to stretch the truth that far against someone. He's only a man for crying out loud, no more, no less. He can't control the world, so let's just leave him alone for Pete's sake."

That was the end of Rufus Splatter's story, but not the end of the talk about Harness. Another round of chatter was that when Mack Stems had been gone, a special package arrived for Harness via Pony Express. Seems that a tall, gaunt, worn-out and dusty young man in leather chaps wearing a large ten-gallon hat came galloping in to town to drop off a piece of mail for Harness Trenchold. The man declared, "My God all golly, I hope I'm not too late. Kind of got caught in a flash flood back some fifty years back and I've been searching around for this Harness fella ever since." Then, as quickly as he'd appeared, the man on the horse rode off, disappearing like a red-tailed hawk spiraling into early morning light.

This Pony Express story was the work of Don Barnes, a man who claimed to know everything that had happened, did happen, and would happen in Fargas Union. Don, who was about seventy years of age, spent most of his time sitting, eating and talking. This was pretty evident by the large size of his stomach and his two thin legs. At one time Don had been a very important citizen in Fargas Union, but a legal charge that he had abused his wife put his life on hold. The charges were never proved, but that they had been made against him at all caused a great many people in town to never fully trust Don again. Things had changed to his advantage, however, now that his wife had passed on. No further complaints were ever made against him.

Don said he couldn't believe his eyes when the horse came roaring up to the post office doors. And as Don was prone to doing, and for that matter expected to do, he tried to explain the mystery in his own assumptive and fictitiously crackpot manner. He began declaring with a confident and verbose demeanor to anyone who would listen, "If that Trenchold ain't got some trick up his sleeve, then I must be a cackling crow doing flips in the air. Watching a lone cowboy come waltzing into our town on a horse and delivering mail ought to make anyone know a thing ain't any no more square than a circle. That man out on the edge of town is a voodoo doll in disguise. He's aiming to take over the world. That's right, aiming to take over and rule THE WORLD!"

"You done said a mouthful of truth with that one there, Donnie. That man must be a queer or my name ain't Georgie Buck Able," chimed in Georgie Buck Able, Don's trusty, no-brained, rail-thin, tobacco-chewing and longtime sidekick of conversation. Georgie always championed each and every phrase uttered by Don, like a loyal and well-paid servant.

Don puffed up and went on to add a little more on Harness: "I do believe there's a chance Mr. Trenchold can toss bodies the way a ventriloquist can throw a voice. He's no dummy; he's a red scare, I tell you! A rusted and evil, no-good-for-nothing, tarnished red-faced scarecrow."

"Donnie Don, I do believe you pinned the tail on the donkey's ass this time, yes sir. I think you stuck that tail on the butt of the ol' bullseye," spurted a lightly trembling Georgie Buck Able.

So what was missing from all this talk? Well, once again it was the presence of any evidence. When Don was asked by Abraham Dewlink for a detail or two more, Don balked and answered he couldn't rightly recall anymore at this particular instant, but so help him God, he had told the truth! In fact, if Abraham wanted to come back tomorrow, he'd be able to tell him everything, even the horse's hoof size. "For chrissakes," he said, "haven't I lived long enough that my word stands for anything around here? My word's as good as gold; you know that, Abraham Dewlink!"

"With the wind as my witness, I believe you, Donnie," chimed in Georgie Buck Able. "I believe you got the wick in the gunpowder this time." Georgie grinned and looked back and forth from Abraham to Don, smiling a wide and happy grin.

Chapter Four

But where had Harness come from? If anyone had bothered to ask Harness himself, this is what he would have been told: Harness found the site for Pick Up Stick City during three years of crisscrossing travel.

The story has many parts to it. At first he wasn't necessarily in search of a ghost town, just freedom and isolation. Then, after exploring his mind and the land and his personal ideas about what made a good life, he came to the conclusion that what he wanted to do was become engrossed in restoration. The cliché of "going west" seemed totally worn out and senseless to him.

He was tired of avoiding the dark and scary regions of the world. He was curious why everyone had either jumped past the center of the country or abused the Midwestern regions and left. He didn't want to try and strike it rich in creamy, clear and calm virginity amongst the giant growth of redwood trees and the easy flight of condors. He preferred the foraging quality of a wild turkey, the resurrection of peregrine falcons.

He felt a sense of compassion, too. He hated that people had destroyed the Midwestern topsoil and left it behind, that everyone wanted to poke fun at Midwesterners for their innocence, their mild landscape, their slow lives. For the most part it was true; Midwesterners had been duped, tricked and screwed over, but they hadn't lost their imagination. Living well in the area, in fact, actually required it. Imagination wasn't so hard to come by he often thought, when you lived by mountains and oceans and bears. One takes wonder for granted when the popular version of the sublime is right out your front door. Harness, as if an old monk, wanted to work on rising with the sun and setting with the sun, entrenching himself in patience, which he knew would result in slow motion miracles So, calmly, he began.

Harness declared as his personal motto: "I will bring back the worn and the trashed, the overlooked and the dirty!" Harness handwrote this saying on a piece of paper and thumbtacked it to the roof of his truck. This happened a couple of years prior to finding Pick Up Stick City. The saying served as a constant reminder for his quest in life. Knowing what he wanted changed Harness. He stopped being so sarcastic all the time and, instead, became honest about what he expected and wanted of the world.

Although he knew the virtue of patience, searching for the right place had been a long three years. He had spent his time going from one small town to another, talking and listening to the elderly men at hardware stores in Nebraska, keeping his ears open while attending auctions in Minnesota, eavesdropping at truck stops in Wyoming. He'd spent hours reading classified ads in newspapers and looking through old magazines in antique stores, all the while hoping to find some old property where the hustle and bustle of life had once existed and needed to be recovered.

One day he heard about a ghost town that interested him from an old lady named Maeline Tab at a Volunteer Fire Department's fundraising chili dinner in northeastern South Dakota near the Big Sioux River. She told Harness, "I had a second cousin who lived in a remote village, somewhere southeast of here in northern Iowa." Maeline explained, "The town, I was told, had a sixty-foot waterfall and was wonderfully set beside a clear and flowing picturesque stream." She explained that these relatives of hers had all either moved, died, or even possibly drowned over the years until, one day, nothing had been left but rubble and memories. "We weren't the closest family, so I never heard what happened to any of them for certain. Just none of us, including my mother or father, ever heard from them again. We assumed they left for Alaska or something; 'course by now they'd have all passed away."

Harness liked the sound of the waterfall, the drownings, the rubble, the mysteries and the memories. He got directions as far as a small village she called Fargas Union. The old lady told him she suspected, once he made it that far, someone could steer him the rest of the way. Harness finished his chili, thanked Maeline, then took off. When he finally pulled into Fargas Union, he asked a couple of old men on a porch for the last few directions out to what was supposed to be the ghost town.

Don Barnes had been the one who'd told Harness the way to Pick Up Stick City in the first place. Don's large stomach rose and fell as he talked, and his grizzly hands kneaded each other furiously when he wasn't talking. "You just gotta go down ol' double D, go left at the big ol' cottonwood with the Darcy's Beauty Bin sign nailed to it, then on through Three Crooked Grin curves. From there just follow the stream to the end. Oughta warn you, though, cowboy, ain't much there. That ol' place could use a good coat of diesel and a match."

"Now that's a good one, Donnie boy, yep, that's a good one for the books for certain, uh-huh, yep, show 'em the way my friend, show him the way," chimed in a wispy, hallow-faced and nervous-looking man sitting next to Don, whose eyes darted from side to side as he listened to Don speak. Harness later learned this was Georgie Buck Able.

"Sounding better all along," Harness mumbled to himself after saying thanks and walking back to his truck.

"That there must be one of them washed-out hippies we been hearing about from time to time. Probably no more than a grinner, though, I'd say, no more than a grinner. You know the kind, Georgie, all afloat with dreams and good vibrations, but swimming in place and smoking that dopey hippie-weed-cabbage stuff I heard about on the radio so much. Always living in their heads and talking about peace and flowers and what-not," commented Don Barnes.

"A jag in a jigsaw puzzle, that's for sure, Donnie, that's for certain-antly sure," added Georgie Buck Able as they watched Harness drive off.

Harness followed Don's directions and knew he had found the ghost town he was looking for as soon as he spotted the old collection of buildings and surrounding landscape.

Chapter Five

The old town was down in a valley, nestled up against a long continuous, steep limestone bluff, which made the area seem hidden from the north. If a spot could be a noise, this old town was a silent spot between a long, drawn-out pattern of echoes. The land around him felt alive and full of stories. Harness walked quietly and silently, careful not to awaken someone. He truly felt, right away, as though the town were merely asleep, not dead. Maybe, just maybe, everyone was simply hibernating.

What transpired next put a hardened clenched knot in the mind and body of Harness and caused him to remain in this spot.

As Harness walked around he noticed a gathering of birds just on the other side of a thick hedgerow of trees, behind one of the old abandoned buildings. All sorts and types of birds seemed to be flying busily about, all carrying sticks, straw, paper, colored flowers, twigs and berries. There were ravens and owls, sparrows and rough-legged hawks, finches, chickadees, downy woodpeckers, indigo buntings, orchard orioles, even one osprey, a wild turkey and a bald eagle. It was such a concentration of action and feathers that Harness couldn't ignore it. He approached the clamor to see what was going on, and as he went around the row of trees, the bunches and flocks of birds spread apart and landed in the trees, on the building tops beside them, and on the ground nearby. They arranged themselves in a type of safe semicircle around him, settling down, waiting quietly like a makeshift audience. Birds always seemed to be near Harness all his life, but he had to admit this did seem odd. After all, he hadn't seen bald eagles, tufted titmice and great blue herons sharing the same area so closely before.

When Harness neared the spot where all the activity had been, he looked down at the ground and understood that angels had sprinkled his life with pure magic. The gods, the spirits, the land, maybe the birds, had spoken, had laid down the daily bread, so to speak. There, before Harness, like a broad romantic landscape painting with a halo in the center, rested the spelling of his name in the dirt.

The birds had written his name with sticks and straw, even created a ring of colored flower petals and berries around it as adornment. Gawking and trembling, Harness smiled and let his shoulders drop comfortably below his neck. He didn't know whether to be joyful or frightened. The birds flew back and clustered near him for a few moments and then, in one big gust, flew their separate ways. Never before had Harness been presented with such a generous offering. To say he suddenly felt at home would have been a tremendous understatement. He would not, could not flinch, waver, or abandon this spot on earth. As though he were a tree, he began to grow roots right then and there.

Not until the sun went behind a tree and cast a shadow over him did Harness think about moving again. And when he did, a sudden gust of wind arrived, blowing his name apart. He smiled and thanked the world and the elements, and any other powers that may be involved, for bringing him here and making this his refuge.

Breathing steadily and using the limits of his eyesight for examination, Harness looked around again as though for the first time. There was some typical trash lying about: a messy stone fire pit, busted beer bottles, chunks of linoleum and light plastic pieces blown into old windows. The corner of one building was crumbling, a whole roof was missing from one of the other buildings, but really, for an old town, the place was perfect. Harness got the sort of feeling that perhaps only a person wanting to own a ghost town would feel right away: feelings of memory and loads of potential, resting calmly about. He felt as though he were standing in the midst of whispered stories, within lingering earshot of a fading choir of memories.

There was a perfect restoration of nature, as well. Weeds were growing through the middle of bricks, and birds had taken to nesting in old baseball caps. These returns to nature told Harness that the place was pure as a compost pile, not covered in asbestos, or motor oil and diesel, not clotted with deep and deadly long-lasting chemical-disaster compounds. Instead, items were shapeshifting back to dirt. The phrase "ashes to ashes, dust to dust," went through his mind. This place could be viewed as much an ending as a place to begin.

Remembering Maeline Tab's words about a waterfall, Harness set out to explore. There wasn't much chance of getting lost since the area was neither big enough nor was Harness concerned enough to feel lost. The town was a cluster of three old limestone buildings, four weather-beaten, wooden-framed homes, plus one brick structure. When imagined from overhead, the place was no more than a street corner, four city blocks, sharing one center—one block east, west, north and south. To the northwest of the center of the town Harness found water falling over the steep bank that surrounded the town, dwarfing its size in the landscape. Beneath the waterfall rested a giant pool of water, thirty feet around and what looked to be just as deep. The pool of water flowed easterly out of town. The river was contained on one side by the steep bluff of limestone, an embankment so tall that Harness couldn't see beyond the edge of the town. He stood in a fold in the land.

Harness walked over to where he could see the river better, where he could view the beauty of the falls. A slow-motion flow of water dropped from above his head, through the air, like strands of tall big bluestem prairie grass moving back and forth in the wind. Most of the water converged onto a moss-covered boulder, where a rounded cavity captured the water, swirling it together before it continued bubbling downstream in slow moving whirlpools. Walking to the edge of the pool, Harness scared a few trout that were feeding on small insects near the water's surface.

Harness grinned. Yes, everything he'd been looking for was here. Limestone buildings, bricks, old native hardwoods, river water, trout, isolation and memories— not to mention a sublime welcome mat from the resident birds. As Harness looked into the water, his mind began to drift and daydream. This tumbled down place, this Pick Up Stick City, would be his home. His search was over.

As the moon rose that night, Harness pushed the mattress he kept in the rear of his truck to the ground, ate some dinner and then lay down. Looking at the night sky, he felt an easy sense of place, a rare moment of calmness. He felt that who he was and wanted to be and could be had begun to come true. For the first time in a long while he didn't dream at all during the night. He didn't have to anymore. He had begun to live his dream.

Chapter Six

When the sun rose the next day and the existence of the ghost town turned out to be real, Harness wanted to start restoring and exploring right away. He strolled over and admired what remained of his name that the birds had designed. Then he began to stack some old wood into piles that were laying around the foundation of what he noticed was an old store, a faded sign reading "Ponderlink's Grocery." Harness knew he would have to take care of some business before he got carried away, though. He had to find a seller and go through the process of land rights and ownership in order to tie everything together. Selfish, perhaps, but Harness wanted to know that he had a right to the land before he began to make changes and explore. Harness readied himself for the drive into Fargas Union.

Not knowing where to go for information about buying land, when Harness got to town he went to the Fargas Union post office. From earlier drives around the Midwest, Harness had learned one place that always had a person with information and a decent smile was at the post office. Harness found the office in Fargas Union without much trouble. He walked in and struck up a conversation as best he could.

"… information like what?" asked the clerk.

"Like whether the place is for sale," said Harness.

"That old spot? You know it's no more than a pile of bricks and a bunch of bad water, don't you?" said the clerk.

"Yes, I guess I do, but I still wouldn't mind knowing more all the same, if you don't think anyone would mind?" replied Harness.

"Well, I'd say that if you want that old place bad enough, I can't imagine why you couldn't work something out. Tell you what, why don't you just leave your name with me, and I'll get the word to Jack Busby. Jack would have to be the one to sell the place to you and, well, I know he's not around now. But I'll tell him about you. It's not like I could forget. Haven't had a person mention buying anything around here for years. You thinking of moving in or something?"

"Likely. At least that's what I'd like to do," Harness said, trying to be vague.

"Now, what'd you say your name was again?" asked the clerk.

"Harness. Harness Trenchold."

"Good. That's good. Mine's Mack Stems. So, like I said, I'll get ol' Jack to see you about the place. Only other thing I'll need to know is where you'll be best found," asked Mack.

"I guess I'll just be out at the old town," answered Harness.

"All righty then, Mr. Trenchold. You just wait around, and Jack'll come on by. I'm sure of that. You come on by if anything changes 'til then," said Mack.

Harness thanked Mack, returned to his truck and began the drive back. So far it seemed easier than he thought.

As Harness left the post office, Mack Stems thought about Harness. He was certainly curious. What kind of person wants to buy an old ghost town? It isn't so unusual to explore ruins, to meander through graveyards examining tombstones, or just being drawn to quirky old places for a short period of time. But it seemed strange to Mack for someone, an adult no less, to show up one day and want to purchase a place that had commonly been known of as no more than rubble. The old town was a place where people had failed at life; it was not a place to begin again. Of course, Mack Stems didn't know a whole lot about Harness, either.

*****

It was nearly eight days before Mack Stems got in touch with Jack Busby.

"You say he wants what?" asked a surprised Jack Busby when Mack told him the news.

"Well, just like I said, he wants the old Siren Falls," repeated Mack Stems.

"Did you bother to tell him that the place ain't much more than a pile of bricks and a pool of bad water?"

"Yep, told him all that, didn't flinch a bit. In fact, he's living out there now. He told me he'd be waiting to hear from you," Mack answered.

"Well, if he's waiting, I suppose I'd better get to finding the land titles and figure out some sort of offer. Did he mention anything about money, or prices?" asked Jack.

"Didn't utter a peep, but then he didn't seem to be thinking much about money. He just acted very interested in the place is all. I'll say this as well; he doesn't seem to just be passing through, either. Something about him seems serious and intent."

"Well, then, all right, if you see this guy, this, what's his name again?" asked Jack.

"Harness. Harness Trenchold."

"Okay, then, if you see Mr. Harness Trenchold before I do, let him know I'm on my way."

"All righty, Jack, if I see him I'll let him know," said Mack.

Chapter Seven

When Jack Busby finally showed up at Pick Up Stick City to see Harness, it was a surprise for them both. Harness was trying to coax a queen ant out of the ground with a drop of honey he'd placed on the end of a cottonwood stick. If it weren't for Jack's commitment to standard protocol, manners and politeness, he would have turned around right away.

Jack walked up to Harness as he was kneeled over the ground yelling at the mound of dirt where the ants lived. Harness looked up and, as naturally as possible, stood, knocked the dirt off his clothes, kicked the ground and tried to think of something reasonable to say.

"Hey, there," started Harness, "guess you caught me spying on some ants. You must be Mack's friend coming out about the land?"

Offering his hand, Jack started talking, "Busby, Jack Busby, spoke with Mack the other day, in fact. How are you, Harness? Yes sir, the red ant can get a man bad, no doubt about that, I've always said. So you want to buy this old place, I understand? Now, not a bad idea. It's got a lot to offer a person like yourself, I'd imagine. Didn't mean to take so long getting to you, but I had to do some research on the old place, you understand. It's for sale, though, that's for sure, and I suppose that's all you really want to know. Just to let you know the gist of the matter, so you know it's all legal. I mean, apparently the city titles merged into a sort of common estate—normal enough, perfectly normal in these parts—making it a case of abandonment, making a consolidation possible, you might say. In the long run I just had to decipher through a series of county zoning clauses regarding the proper method of ownership…"

Harness was having a rough time following along with Jack's words, having to look into his eyes, needing to nod at just the right times. He'd never been accustomed to social skills. His slow and isolated lifestyle made simple human interactions a chore. He knew he was behaving sluggishly and missing most of what Jack was saying and was just glad Jack didn't stop talking because it gave him time to figure out what was going on.

Jack Busby, on the other hand, was simply talking because he was too nervous to stop. He had the feeling that Harness had no idea what he was saying. To Jack, it felt like he was talking to an acorn and would have to wait for the entire oak tree to grow before he was understood. Harness' eyes were glazing over, and Jack found himself saying anything he could think of, watching Harness for some indication of responsiveness. Jack mentioned again that the town was for sale and saw that this comment seemed to click somewhere inside Harness' head; there was a bit of a flash in his eyes.

Jack Busby considered himself to be a very plain man. He was interested in very few things. He wasn't really bored with his life, but he had no passion for anything in particular. He liked talking to people about small things: the weather, baseball, gardens. About the only thing Jack felt competent at was selling real estate. The main attraction to the whole business for Jack was imagining the way people would live out their lives on the real estate he sold them. He wanted things to be like the fairy tales that had happily-ever-after endings. He was having a hard time with Harness. He'd been expecting a more enterprising person, a man who wanted to prosper financially, or maybe someone who wanted a Hollywood set to film a movie. Harness seemed more like one of the modern artists his rich oil-baron, conservative Uncle Earlis had told him about—the kind of person who took long naps and did sloppy renditions of white-on-white snowstorms rather than someone who was interested in real estate investment. Jack never thought that, in his life time, anyway, he'd meet a man sitting on the ground yelling at an ant bed.

Jack continued on, "…I have consolidated this whole area, and it can be purchased using a noncommercial deed. This really only matters as far as property taxes go. Basically what all this boils down to, for your sake, Harness, is that we'll just need to figure out what price it's all going to go for. Now, what I was thinking, the place being in such poor condition and all was …"

The only thing Harness had heard the entire time Jack Busby had been talking was the part about the place being for sale. That's all he cared about. When he heard Jack mention determining a price, he quickly interrupted.

"I'll just pay you right now, Mr. Busby. Hold on. It's my pleasure. Good work like yours deserves to be rewarded." Harness walked over to his truck and got out 25 packets of traveler's checks. He handed them to Jack. "Here, this should be enough to pay for the land and give you a pretty penny for all the work you did me. Here, now, go ahead, take this money. Take it. I don't know how to thank you enough."

Slightly unnerved, Jack stood back a bit and held out his arms. "Now hold on here, Harness. This is land we're talking about, not some sort of small-time purchase you just write a check for. I don't know what price we'll agree at, but we should make a contract, don't you think? I believe in doing things properly, albeit with due speed for your benefit as much as mine …"

"Please Mr. Busby, just go ahead and take the money. I don't know any better way to do this," interrupted Harness.

Jack was just a bit irritated. He wasn't used to such odd behavior. Taking up one of the packets of traveler's checks Harness handed him, he paused. Each check was worth $250.00. There were twenty checks to a packet. Jack did the math in his head, looked at Harness for a second, then looked back down at the checks. "I don't know if we should do this. I mean, it isn't fair for you to pay this much. I couldn't in good faith take this much money for the place. It isn't much more than a pile of busted-up stones and bricks, Mr. Trenchold. Half of this would be too much." Jack tried to give the money back.

"Jack, I don't want to sound mean, but this place is a whole lot more than just a pile of bricks to me. I guess what I'm trying to say is we're not negotiating so much as I'm paying you. Here, let me countersign those checks, and if you'll write up a real simple agreement for each of us, we can finish this whole thing right now, okay?"

Jack was still befuddled. "No, Harness, no, that's not what I meant. I mean, I didn't mean that this place is literally a pile of bricks. It's just that no one has really had any interest in this spot for so long, you know? It's easy to misunderstand what can be right in front of our eyes sometimes, you know how it is?"

"Not really," said Harness. He was starting to feel anxious. He just wanted to countersign the checks and get everything over with. He didn't know if he could continue to behave as a normal member of society much longer. His nerves were beginning to unravel, his body was sweating, and his shoulders were becoming tense.

"Okay, then, okay, if I don't have a choice. I'll say one thing, though, this is pretty unusual. Do you have any plans for old Siren Falls, or what?" asked Jack Busby.

Harness held out his hand and said, "Well, Jack, I'm just planning on fixing things up and making some friends." He paused. "So, do we have a deal?"

The two men shook hands, and Jack added, "Deal. You just come on in to Fargas Union in a week or so and pick up the title to the place at the post office. I'll tell Mack and see to it that he has you sign all the dotted lines. Glad you're happy, Mr. Trenchold. I'll look forward to hearing from you now and then as well, you hear?" said Jack.

As Jack Busby drove off, he tried hard to make sense of what had happened. He felt guilty, anxious and nervous all over. He'd never made such a deal before. The speed of the sale made him feel like a small child; he was all twitchy and excited. Everything had been such a surprise. After driving a few minutes, he pulled to the edge of the road, got out the traveler's checks, and counted them. He started laughing hysterically. "What a crazy dumb-ass bastard," he yelled. "What a crazy, freaking lunatic!"

As Harness watched Jack Busby drive off, he knew that in just a couple of minutes, Jack would be thinking that he was totally crazy for paying so much money for what everyone seemed to think was basically a worthless heap of junk. Harness hated bickering over prices and contracts. He knew he wanted to buy this place and just decided to offer way too much money for it and get it over with. In Harness' mind the money he had given was nothing compared to what he now had. He now owned his dream.

Chapter Eight

The story of how Harness came upon all his money is worth telling. It isn't the usual script for wealth, that's for sure. Harness had come into the world a wealthy man, having been conceived as a bet in the city of Sparks, way out west in the sometimes state of mind called Nevada.

His mother was a pure and simple gambler and believed that money, as well as life and emotion, was either lost or found, quick as slick greasy grass. One night she had gambled with her body. She'd heard about a man in Las Vegas who said no matter the lady, no matter what day of the month, angle of the sun, placement of the moon, or type of blood, a child born of his love would be a girl. He'd put money on it. When Harness' mother walked up and challenged the man, he told her she'd be wasting her money as he was made of female genes through and through. He believed in himself so strongly he was willing to bet two million dollars this time.

Harness' mother couldn't resist. She bet the man, made an evening of it and waited for the results. Rumor had it that the man really just liked to sleep around, but, even so, he hadn't lost a bet of this sort for well over ten years. He'd been involved in the birth of twenty-four girls and had earned himself nearly thirty million dollars.

The birth of Harness speaks for itself. He was worth two million dollars the instant he was born. Harness' mother put the whole two million in the bank and let it grow. He was the lucky one; his three little sisters had cost his mother six million dollars. A fourth sister would have cost Harness' mother double or nothing, except that his mother passed away one month into her pregnancy, so no one bothered to figure out what sex she'd been carrying as, no matter the sex, it would have been bittersweet.

By the time his mother died, Harness was seventeen years old and ready to begin his life alone. Harness never knew his sisters since they had all been sent away for adoption by his mother when they turned out to be girls. "I couldn't possibly love them after what they did to me," Harness' mother told him when he asked where they went.

Aware that he was financially secure as soon as he could comprehend adult conversation, Harness spent his life searching for strange and sumptuous ideas to entertain himself with. It was rare for him to spend more than six days inside the walls of an organized school during a school year, so because he'd never passed a grade of school his entire life, he was fourteen years old, sitting in a kindergarten class room, before he finally walked away from organized schooling for the last time.

He wasn't lacking in education, however. When Harness turned eight he could easily read, do math and all the stuff that schools seemed to think were so hard and important. By the age of twelve he was well on his way to discovering how to make a ladder out of raindrops so that he could climb up in the sky during a rainstorm. At age fifteen Harness had mastered cloud sculpture and was trapping thunder inside canning jars. By not going to school, Harness was able to learn things that most people had no idea could even be thought of. Harness was opposed to learning what everyone else was learning. He declared that what people were learning in school amounted to no more than brainwashing. Harness was lucky and he realized it. He knew he was fortunate to have the chance to really study the world and not get lost in the patterns and repetitions of normal life. As he progressed in years, one of his favorite comments became, "Surprise is knowledge's victory." It became clear, as soon as he found Pick Up Stick City, that all of his self-taught education would be vital.

*****

For a good period of time Harness was truly the center of conversation in Fargas Union. However, credit really should have gone to Jack Busby for keeping most of the talk to nothing more than speculation and confusion. Jack had kept the excessive payment for the old pile of bricks to himself. In fact, he had placed all the checks into hiding and only used them when he went out of town. He knew it wouldn't be too good if word got out about the wealth Harness possessed, not to mention that people wouldn't like a stranger who could buy whatever he wanted, whenever he wanted. People can get wicked when something easy happens for a person, especially when it's a stranger. It's dirt in the eyes and blood in the lungs that people want to hear about, not instant success stories. In addition, folks would pretty much hate Jack if they found out how much of a profit he'd made.

Since no one was really sure what was going on with Harness, folks went around making things up: putting words and ideas to the wind, then falling for their own bait, saying that Harness had done this and Harness had done that. Eventually people got tired of speculation, but not at first. At first it was fun having a person to try and figure out.

The folks in Fargas Union predicted a wide variety of possibilities about Harness: that he was opening a drive-in movie theater, a power plant, a brothel, a church, even a white asparagus farm. Although none of the rumors ended up being the truth, they became a problem for Harness because people actually went to the trouble to check them out.

Even a longshot guess would get someone's attention. It usually went like this: Polly Patterson would tell Aunt Mar that she'd heard Harness had just received a mail-order degree in divinity and was opening his own Church of the Wolverine, with readings and liturgy from something called the Wild Testament on Sunday. Then Aunt Mar would tell her daughter-in-law Judy Pitstream, and Judy naturally told Joe Mahrees who would tell Clint Rim. Then, since Clint Rim was only eighteen and bored to tears with his life in Fargas Union, he'd gotten together with his friends Timmy Slickrock and Rudi Liptaut and driven out to Pick Up Stick City the first Sunday following the hearsay to check things out. Once there, they'd walked up to the building by Harness' truck, knocked on the door and asked when church was going to start.

To which Harness had replied, "It's not being held today, or any day, boys." It was irritating, but that was that.

At some point in time, during the passing of the seasons, over the course of several years, the people in Fargas Union finally got tired of trying to figure out what Harness was up to. The only talk that persisted was how little difference Harness actually made. In some ways the people of Fargas Union were relieved that Harness wasn't a threat to them, but at the same time they were also disappointed that he hadn't made a difference. It would have been nice, most people agreed, if Harness had given them something more than next to nothing. Don Barnes summed it up best: "That boy out there ain't no more than a ghost himself. I tell you something, it's a crying shame to get something and end up with nothing."

"Yes, sir, yessiree, you're right again there Donnie boy, right again, right on the money, my friendly friend friend," chimed in Georgie Buck Able.

Don went on, "I wonder if that ol' boy ain't got something planned for Halloween, being so much a relative to ghosts and all?" This actually scared Georgie Buck Able for a second, and he didn't respond right away to this comment since Don was known to have a way with premonitions.

"By and by I sure hope you aren't right, Donnie. I sure to heck hope you're not right this time there, my friend," uttered Georgie Buck Able.

"Don't you worry none there, Georgie. We'll be okay," Don said with a smile.

"Oh no no no, not me Donnie, not me, I'm not worried, I'm not scared, Donnie! I believe you pinned that donkey's hind end again, that's all, you pinned the donkey a good one this time," Georgie Buck Able said with big broad grin, swatting at the back of his neck a couple of times until he stopped moving and said, "Yessiree, you've got it right again, good buddy."

Chapter Nine

A number of months after officially buying Pick Up Stick City, Harness drove into Fargas Union to see Mack Stems at the post office.

"Hiya, Mack," said Harness.

"Hiya, Harness. Come for the title to your land? If so, 'bout time I'd say," asked Mack.

"Well, not really, but I'll get the papers, I suppose. What I really want, though, is a post office box, if you've got one," answered Harness.

"If that's what you're wanting, then you've come to the right spot. I don't even charge. Hoping for some mail, are you?"

"Could be, not sure. I get a letter every six-seven years," replied Harness with a lighthearted chuckle.

"Have a number preference, or will you take any number?" asked Mack.

"Anything you've got," answered Harness.

"Sixty-seven, then, right on the end there," stated Mack.

"That'll be just what I need," said Harness.

"Fine by me. Well, then, I'll tell you what I tell all the others and that's we get mail on Tuesday and Thursday. Only I wouldn't recommend checking until Thursday since, in my opinion, we don't get all we have coming to us on Tuesday. I'm pretty certain that they load up extra during the week to make Thursday seem extra important, it being toward the end of the week and all," Mack explained.

"All right Mack, thanks a lot," Harness said.

"The ol' ghost town coming along okay?" asked Mack as Harness was just about to leave.

"Yep, it's becoming a masterpiece."

"All righty then, Harness, see you sometime later," said Mack.

*****

It was the water that was really making Harness excited about Pick Up Stick City and, in part, what caused Harness to go open a post office box. When Harness first saw the waterfall, he knew there was the potential for something spectacular. Everyone kept saying that the place was a pile of bricks and a bunch of bad water. Well, people must not have been out to the waterfall in a while, because the river was brimming with trout and clear as early autumn air. Harness knew trout couldn't live in a badly contaminated spot, and he drank heartily of the water each day, splashing the cold liquid on his face in the mornings to wake up, using it as mouthwash to prevent cavities. It was obvious, from all the rusty items he pulled from the water, along with all the dead weeds he removed, that at some point pollution had been a major problem. Yet, for whatever reason, probably just disregard, the water had come back to life.

One day, while Harness was lifting old decay out of the pool, down at the bottom of it was a large pile of small egg-looking rocks. Each stone was slightly smaller than a chicken's egg. Harness was intrigued by the white stones, and one night he had a dream that the stones could be incubated and hatched. The very next morning Harness swam down into the cold pool and, looking through the clear water, gathered five of the whitish stones. He pulled them out of the water and placed them on the ground in a small pile a few feet from the shore.

Harness thought over the possibility of hatching pieces of rock. Would he shatter them with a hammer, or perhaps plant them in the ground as seeds? He wasn't sure. Convinced he needed time to figure out what to do, he left the stones piled on the ground and went back to cleaning out the pool of water, as he had been doing the day before.

When Harness returned to the pile of stones later in the day, once again surprise became a blessing and a source of knowledge. Harness discovered that the stones really were eggs. When the sun had shone all day on the five eggs he had pulled out, they'd begun to crack open and transform as they dried. Squatting down for a closer look, Harness picked them up, one by one, and saw that on the hollow inside of each white stone was a relic of a particular person's life from the town: a saved baby tooth, old love letters, locks of hair, newspaper clippings regarding a person's brief moment of fame. One of the notes he discovered caused Harness to shudder with the concepts of premonitions and soothsaying.

A little handwritten note on a small piece paper, no more than an inch and a half long, about half an inch tall, similar to a fortune cookie note, read:

"Save me from the elements! Return me if found! Sincerely, Mr. Morgan Bullwhip, In Care Of: Mr. Harness Trenchold, Pick Up Stick City, Heartland, USA."

This note was the reason Harness went to town and opened the post office box. How could anyone know that this place existed, that he was here now, and had named it Pick Up Stick City? That these few details were contained inside a stone beneath the water left him with no clear explanation. Harness thought it over, but he simply couldn't explain it, unless there were some spirit, someone, who knew he existed and knew what he was doing here.

It was days before Harness recovered from the discovery of the items in the stones. Not knowing what to do, he left the stones alone, staring at them if he walked by, wondering. A few days later he noticed the stones were gone. He thought that maybe some birds had flown off with them but observed, instead, that they were up the shoreline a piece, barely covered by water.

Harness walked over to where the eggs now lay and decided it was time to test a theory he'd been pondering: he was going to try and hatch some eggs himself. Gathering up the stones from the shoreline, he then swam down to get four more stones to add to the collection. Then Harness tried something way beyond strange, even for him. He glued some feathers he had found to the seat of his pants, formed a nest with some clumps of long dry grass, placed the small white stones inside the nest and sat down on them like a chicken. He knew he probably looked like he had completely lost his mind, but he had a theory rolling around in his head, and if he didn't try this idea, he'd never know what might happen. He ruffled his arms, muttered a couple of "bock-bocks," and settled in.

Harness sat like a bird for nearly four days, placing a thick wool blanket over the nest when he left for any length of time. It was during the middle of the third day that he felt the bottom of his pants getting wet. Standing up he saw that the white stones were beginning to grow in size. Each had doubled and become slightly moist on the outside. Harness brushed the water off his rear and sat back down. The thought that this idea to hatch the stones may work seemed outrageous, but he stayed on the nest for the rest of the day and into the night.

The next day, as the yolky-looking sun began to rise, Harness not only had a wet behind but a hot one. As he slowly began to unwind his stiff legs and stand off the eggs, he knelt over to have a look at what was happening. The eggs were slowly melting and becoming puddles of waxy water. He examined this transformation up close, and, with his face near the waxy-surfaced water, heard something. He put one of his ears up near a particular stone, which he thought was talking. There was not a voice, precisely, but definitely a noise, such as the updraft of a wood stove burning.

A little disappointed that the stones hadn't given birth to a more solid form of life, he took a step back from the puddle that had formed, but when he looked into the water again he saw more than just his reflection. He saw what appeared to be people living amongst the buildings he recognized as being those of this very town. Harness suddenly knew, as though it were the most natural thing in the world, that there were stories, legends, myths, even lives, hidden inside the small stones he was pulling out of the water.

Not exactly sure how to contain the images in the water, Harness did the first thing that came to his mind: he rolled the waxy surface of the puddle up and made a candle with the aid of a piece of string he had in his pocket. He then stomped into the water that was left and laughed out loud, holding the curious candle high above his head. There has to be a reason for this, he reasoned, a sort of message in a bottle, just like people he used to read about when he was little.

Time seemed to be evaporating around Harness. As he pulled the candle back down to his side, he realized he was hungry and that the sun was already setting. But before he got ready to leave and go inside, Harness took another look at the water that was left. His instincts told him that this couldn't be normal water, it just couldn't be, and that it may be as close to truly tasting holy water as he'd ever get in his life. Kneeling over like a deer, he sipped the water cautiously, slowly. It was quite warm and gritty.

He considered getting a jar to store the remaining water, but when he looked down at the puddle again, it had all vanished.

The last rays of sunlight filtered over the landscape, and Harness went inside the old grocery store he was currently living in and lit the candle he had made. The burning candle gave off an old, musty aroma that reminded him of the water he had tasted in the puddle. The flickering flame cast a strange and subdued light into the room, and after his eyes got used to the room's hue, he noticed that there was a series of shadows cast on the ceiling, like a puppet show. These shadows must be a story of some sort, Harness thought. He lay down on the hard wooden floor and watched the ceiling, hoping he could make sense of what he saw.

He watched and he watched. The candle burned for over three hours, and yet he could never put his mind around what it all meant. Were the images he had seen something that had been trapped in the sun, lost in an eclipse, or buried during a flood?

As dawn arrived, his frustration became too heavy to deal with, so he snuffed out the candle and slept. As with all things in Harness' life, he realized that time would translate what it all meant, and time was something he had plenty of.

Chapter Ten

Harness spent every waking hour removing nails, straightening screws, restacking bricks, chopping wood, reinforcing roofs and growing food. He had centered all his attention on the old grocery store at first, since that was to be his new home, and, besides, it only had one really bad spot that needed immediate repair—maybe two or three feet of the main ridge of the roof, nothing bad enough to have caused any major problems in the rest of the structure, and it still had solid oak floors, a reliable chimney system. Even most of the ornate wooden balusters around the front porch area were intact. The original cast iron stove was still in working condition and, with its thick sides, would prove quite valuable when he needed to knock the chill out of the winter air. The brick walls of the store had some blistering, a bit of bowing and some large holes, but nothing some plastering and masonry work couldn't cure. With hard labor and by using lumber, screws, hinges and other odds and ends he found around town, Harness was able to replace and repair the old grocery store to suit his needs.

Each night he slept like a baby, everything was so perfect. His garden was always well-watered, the river was filled with trout, and the orchard gave him fruit. Truly, he felt as though he were in the Garden of Eden. If he had a problem, it was a small one: it was the mystery of what the shadows from the candle meant.

As if he were a farmer harvesting new ideas, Harness found that he was busy with more than restoring buildings. He'd become involved with a whole new chore he'd never expected. He was busy restoring the previous people of the town as well. Almost immediately after the egg-hatching incident, Harness felt that there were people, not exactly dead or alive, lingering and hoping to come back to life all around Pick Up Stick City. He sensed it in the shadows and in the foggy shapes following him out of the corners of his eyes. He had also begun to hear messages in the wind. He began spending more and more time trying to decipher his entire environment; no detail was insignificant. He realized it may all be some form of contagious magic, yet whatever was happening was real. So he began panning his life as though searching for gold, listening to the earth for heartbeats.

It wasn't easy, spotting images all about. Harness constantly felt as though he were looking the wrong direction when it came to spotting what the spirits around him were doing. Some evenings, while sitting outside at a fire, he would look beyond the sparks drifting up into the air and see eyes looking back at him. Some mornings, lying in bed, waiting to get up, he might hear what sounded like a group of people talking, or the sound of music being played at a square dance on the street. Standing in a field, peering deeply into the air occasionally revealed shapes and figures, rings of dancers in celebration. One evening Harness could have sworn that he heard a choir of older ladies singing a song while the sunset illuminated streaks of orange, red and violet. All of this caused him to ponder: was he surrounded by some sort of a land-locked congregation of ghosts?

It seemed to Harness that all of the noises and eyes and clues he was vaguely discerning wanted to be noticed. He trusted this notion because, shortly after the hatching of the eggs, he started finding small handwritten notes all around town, in cabinets, on plates, beside him when he woke up in the morning, even. The first few notes made absolutely no sense at all.

The first note said, "Beware of the vultures perching underneath the long rim of Fulcrum Spinright's straw hat." The second note, from a Florence MacDarts, said, "In the out door, out the side door, find us a better door to come back out of." The third, "We can hide, we can peek, but soon we'll re-emerge, just you wait--your soon to be friend--Billy Baldburton." After the first five or six notes, however, they started making more and more sense to Harness. He credited himself with becoming fluent in the realm of the odd. And just as likely, he thought, the previous residents were probably becoming more comfortable with him as well. He collected the notes in an old box. One by one, each was beginning to tell a story, introducing him to the townsfolks of times past.

Things really shifted the day one of the notes appeared by his side and declared, "Would you stop a moment to eat and drink? Your friend, Ms. Rubia." As a matter of fact, he realized, having worked nearly seven hours straight on the plaster wall in the old bank building, he really was worn out. He took a drink of water, ate some food and felt immensely recovered. In his mind he thanked Ms. Rubia.

One morning, walking down to the pool of water and the waterfall, Harness found a note inside an old beer bottle that read, "Go quickly, save us from the box." Harness thought about this for a second. *What box? Where?* And then he remembered: he hadn't been back to Fargas Union in awhile, not since he had asked Mack Stems to open up a post office box for him. He knew he needed to go to Fargas Union right away.

Chapter Eleven

Harness didn't enjoy coming to town. The only person he was able to tolerate was Mack Stems. Not only had Mack helped out when he'd wanted to buy Pick Up Stick City, but he seemed like a very familiar person who honored another, regardless of what they did. Mack seemed to respect and understand Harness' wish for privacy.

"Well well well if it ain't the Captain. Boy-o-boy, am I glad to see you," Mack bellowed as Harness walked up to the front desk.

Harness could instantly sense an uneasiness in Mack's voice. He had never been this excited to see him before. Harness didn't allow himself to behave anxiously though. Feeling alarmed in Fargas Union was something he avoided at all costs. "Hiya Mack. Uh, any mail laying around for me?" he asked.

"Well, to tell you the truth, Harness," started Mack, looking around to make sure no one else was close by, "as a matter of damn fact, you do have some something in your mailbox. I was getting to where I didn't know if you'd ever come back. You've got a devil of a schedule, my friend, and that's a fact and a half. Not only do you have mail, you got me worried, and I've lived here my whole life. You sure are full of surprises, my friend," Mack stated, his hands tense and shaking. Mack was visibly upset.

"Something's wrong, ain't it?" uttered Harness.

"Could be, could not be," Mack started, "but before we figure that out, you best go clean out that mailbox, because the thing's making me a nervous bag of bones."

Harness felt like a pile of cold scrambled eggs when he looked inside his post office box. He let his mind run circles for awhile trying to figure out what was going on. He didn't want to act too surprised, especially in front of Mack, but he'd be damned if he had a clue. Without touching anything, Harness peered in and looked closer. Not only were there eggs and a duck call, but a few of the eggs had labels on them, neatly handwritten and addressed to him.

Still looking, without touching anything, Harness gazed at one of the brown eggs, examining the written material up close. The postmark was dated 1902, nearly sixty-five years before he'd even arrived. The only thing he could figure was that it must have been addressed by a fortune teller. Who else could have known that an address for a Mr. Morgan Bullwhip; In Care of: Harness Trenchold Pick Up Stick City, USA would ever exist?

Silence passed between Harness and Mack for a good while, lasting neither more nor less than the span of an eternity. A moth flew near the light in the office, circling around and around the bright light bulb above Mack's desk. Confusion and disbelief reigned.

It was as if whatever and whoever had mailed and delivered the mail had been waiting for this day to arrive. Someone, or something, must have known all along that Harness would appear someday. There was a single note as well, resting alone, separate from one of the eggs. Harness carefully, without touching any of the eggs, slid the note out and read it. It turned out to be more of a riddle than anything else. "You heard the siren from far away. You can hatch us in the whirling water. Just let us drop and let us drink and bring us back to life."

Harness read this out loud, and Mack took on the appearance of a stale prune. His face became drawn in and puckered up. Harness tried to remain calm. He looked over at Mack again.

"Don't look at me. I've never seen anything like it. Never. Don't think I'm setting you up, either; I'm not." Mack said right away.

"By chance, did you ever know a Morgan Bullwhip?" Harness asked.

"No no, no sir," said Mack, "never have and don't imagine I ever will. You may want to grab your land title, too. You know, take everything with you, huh?"

"Uh-huh, don't worry, I'll take it all. It's weird, but I have a feeling these little eggs are full of river water and human blood. I've found other things like these around my place. I mean you wouldn't believe," Harness stopped what he was saying when he saw that Mack was pale as a ghost. He realized that he had to stop his talk and thoughts right then and there.

"I already know they got water. Why, hell, pardon me, but one day I saw water leaking from one of them," said Mack.

"Okay, then, I'll take them home and…" Harness said, as he reached his hand in to grab the eggs.

At the exact second that Harness' fingers touched the first egg, the duck call went off with a horrific blasting honk that left Harness' eardrums banging.

"Holy cow!" yelped Mack as he went running for a corner of the office. Harness was so shocked that he dropped one of the eggs on the ground. The duck call went quiet when the egg hit the floor and burst open. With the piercing squeal of the duck call still in his ears, Harness knelt over and looked at the contents of the egg, which had splattered across the floor. His first thought was that it must have contained some type of concentrated water, because when the mere chicken-sized egg burst open, it seemed nearly a gallon of water spilled across the floor—although, really, the contents appeared more like watered-down glue than water. The puddle was well-defined, hadn't spilled loosely, but spread out in a gelatin-like clump.

"Holy mother of jumping Joseph's dreamcoat!" Harness wailed, while he stepped back and looked over the mess. In the middle of the wet spot was a small, dry piece of paper, seemingly coated in wax, like an egg yolk. Harness reached over and picked up the piece of paper (the duck call moaned). Written on the paper yolk was Mr. Morgan Bullwhip's name again.

"Mack?" asked Harness. "Mack?"

Mack showed his face from behind a corner and in a light clear whisper said, "What happened? Are you okay?"

"Got me. This is totally crazy. You sure you never heard of a Mr. Morgan Bullwhip before?" Harness, without thinking, asked again.

"NO NO NO!" Mack spewed. He was getting nervous, real nervous. The fact that no one came running in when the duck call went off was a moment of good fortune as far as he was concerned. "Harness, I think you best take all this out of here. Something's going on, and I don't want you around here. I think I've been about as nice as I can be, but you just gotta go," continued a ragged-looking Mack.

"I know, I know," murmured Harness. "This is too weird, just too weird, I know. I'm sorry, I just don't know what's going on either."

Mack's brain started working hard. He really did want Harness out of here, but a small part of him wanted to know more. His mind was running through the rumors he'd heard. He flashed a brief memory of something Don Barnes said and wondered if it wasn't true. Maybe Harness was involved in some type of wacko voodoo worship or was a Socialist spy of some kind. He looked Harness over, suspicious and weary.

Harness reached out to pick up another of the eggs, and the duck call went off again. This time Harness purposely dropped the egg on the floor.

Mack's nerves could take it no longer. "What are you doing? Get out! Your mess ain't going to become my mess! You're a nutty, wacky madman, Harness! A wild and crazy madman!" raged Mack, shaking all over.

Harness didn't even hear Mack's scream; rather, he knelt down by the floor. "Do you know," he picked up the paper yolk that came out of the second cracked egg and, without paying attention again to the nerves of Mack, asked, "a Ms. Rubia Garcia Rose?"

"No! For the last time, no, no, I don't," screamed Mack. "What's going on here?!" Mack would have considered calling the sheriff himself, except that Harness genuinely seemed confused as well.

"Jeezus." Harness took a deep breath, then just started muttering noises under his breath. He paused again, untucked his shirt from his pants and made a basket in which to gather the eggs up. "Okay, I promise, really, I promise, I'm going to get these things out of here," added Harness.

Relieved to see Harness getting ready to leave, Mack took a deep breath and asked, "What if you get more of these things delivered?"

"Don't worry, I'll come back soon," Harness said, then added, "Does anyone know about this?"

Calming down more, Mack shrugged his shoulders and shook his head. "Not that I know. Heck, even I don't know how the stuff gets here. From time to time I'll look in your box and there's more eggs than before. One time, Don Barnes swore a package was delivered by Pony Express, but I don't trust much more than the word 'hello' out of Don's mouth and sometimes not even that. I never saw any pony deliver anything, but right about now, Harness, I'll have to admit, Don might be on to something. I sure haven't seen anything like this before. I sure hope it doesn't keep happening."

Harness bent over to pick up the bits and pieces of the two eggs that were littered on the floor. It didn't take long to clean up. When he picked up the nametag of each egg, the shattered egg congealed back together with a mercurial speed that was mindboggling.

Mack and Harness stared at the newly formed eggs, then at each other and just shook their heads. There was nothing left to be said. Harness was at a loss, but tried to act rationally to keep Mack from going berserk. Harness put the duck call, which kept squeaking, on top of the pile of eggs. As he started out the door, he leaned over, grabbed at his shirt and kept the eggs and duck call covered. He hoped the call wouldn't honk.

Harness walked out to his truck with the box, his head bowed down to the ground in silence. It wasn't that he was ashamed, but he felt that too much had been revealed, too quickly, in the wrong places. His world was suddenly out of control. He got in his truck, sat and thought, running ideas through his mind as the engine idled.

He emptied the eggs from his shirt to an empty box on the front seat of his truck, covered them and the duck call with an old dirty towel to keep everything safe. He put his truck in gear and began the drive home. After a few miles of driving, he figured out what the first note on the inside of the egg meant. He remembered that as the water fell off the hollow chunk of granite back at the falls, there was a whirlpool about five inches wide and as much as two feet deep. That must be where the eggs needed to be dropped. What the names would mean, what would become of the eggs, well, that was another thing altogether. Chances were, he would find out after he dropped that first egg into the whirlpool.

When Harness finished thinking this, the duck call beside him let out a terrific honk. Harness lifted the towel and looked at the box. The duck call and the eggs were just as he'd placed them. "Did it honk because I'm on to something?" Harness wondered. Again, the duck call let out another loud bark. Harness pulled over to the side of the road, tied the duck call to a piece of string he had in his shirt pocket, and hung it around his neck. This way, Harness reasoned, whenever he did something right with the collection of mysterious eggs, he would be guided with a loud hoot. As if on cue, the duck call gave forth another loud blast.

Chapter Twelve

Harness pulled into Pick Up Stick City and walked straight over to the pool of water beneath the waterfall to have a look. Yes, there was definitely a whirlpool large enough to drop the eggs into. The duck call let out another honk again. Must be the spot, Harness thought. *Honk!*

Without any hesitation, Harness went to his truck, grabbed the egg with Morgan Bullwhip's name, moved to the edge of the pool, took out the egg he knew to be Mr. Morgan Bullwhip, and let it drop into the hollowed spot of water. At that moment the duck call let out such a loud blast of noise that it approximated the flight of a thousand geese rising in flight together. In fact, the duck call actually blew apart, leaving a hole in Harness' sweatshirt and a small cut on his chest.

With his ears ringing and his heart racing, Harness half expected the egg to explode back out of the water in the form of a genie or a ghostly spirit and speak to him about rapture or something, but when nothing dramatic happened right away, Harness calmed down.

Trying to collect his thoughts, Harness looked at the ground around him and stared in disbelief at the broken duck call spread across the soil. His hopes had been pinned on the call helping him with this odd business. Glancing into the water again, he still couldn't spot anything unusual happening.

He was hungry, worn out and sluggish and could hardly think straight. Everything he started to think about stemmed from the realm of the outlandish. He'd left for Fargas Union in the morning with no more than a strong premonition, only to be confronted by Mack and the strangest of possibilities. He shook his head. How often does a person have a duck call talk back to him for a day?

Harness gazed back into the water one last time. He still couldn't see anything happening but was reluctant to leave. Finally, convinced that nothing was going to change too rapidly, he walked the few blocks back to town and the grocery store. He sat down at the kitchen table and felt the tension of the day slipping off his arms. A heavy sleep fell upon him.

It was barely sunrise when he opened his eyes again. In the distance, he heard what sounded like someone gagging and coughing. He stood up groggy from his deep sleep and walked outside. He heard the sound better. The noise was coming from the pool of water.

"The pool of water, that's right, the whirlpool! It's Morgan Bullwhip!" Walking down the road toward the river, Harness could hear the wheezing, hacking noise even better. As he neared the stream, Harness noticed that even the trout were staring into the whirlpool, as though hypnotized. Looking closely himself, Harness saw that some sort of an object was spinning beneath the water inside the tight confines of the whirlpool. Harness jumped into the water and swam down until he was at the edge of the whirlpool.

Submerged beneath the water, the eerie racket became louder to his ears. Peering more deeply into the whirling water, Harness spotted an arm and a leg sprouting from the egg which had contained Mr. Morgan Bullwhip's name. In a surge of energy, Harness swam back up to the surface as fast as he could, spewed a stream of water from his mouth, gasped for air, and yelled, "Wuu-wee! The Bullwhip's coming to life!"

Shaking and trembling like fire blazing wild in a windstorm, a new idea snapped across Harness' mind. He clambered out of the water totally convinced that no one in this town had ever left, or had ever even died!

They're only asleep, he thought, hibernating. I have been hearing their dreams. This whole town is waiting to be restored back to life!

Harness tried to fathom what it meant to be here, next to a person spinning himself back to life in a river. It's a resurrection of some sort, he reasoned. What else could this be?

What at first seemed to be nothing but a calm empty place had now burst forth in all possible directions.

Harness felt stunned. He understood that he had been picked as the one to bring this place back to life. In fact he had been destined to be here and to do this before he ever arrived.

CHAPTER THIRTEEN

The idea of hatching eggs, of bringing people to life, was making Harness feel hyper and anxious. Never had he expected to spend so much time thinking about people when he set out to restore this ghost town. Yet here he was, obsessed with humans and spirits and names.

Another day and night passed since he had first dropped Morgan Bullwhip in the water. When Harness returned to the whirlpool and peered into the water the third morning he saw that the egg with Mr. Morgan Bullwhip's name was still spinning. The wheezing noise he had awakened to a couple days earlier was now more or less gone. The creation process wasn't going to happen as quickly as he had thought it might, but then not much did happen quickly in the world Harness had come to understand. But he was curious, so he jumped into the water again to get a better idea of what was going on. Mr. Morgan Bullwhip was still growing, no doubt about that. He now had half a face and almost two full legs.

The next day, Harness jumped in the water again. Still, not much had changed. Morgan had developed a few toes, but no ears or mouth. Harness swam out of the water, dried off and ate. The suspense had him all knotted up. He was having trouble occupying himself in the midst of this new discovery. So he stopped hanging out by the pool waiting. He made himself leave and thought about doing some tuck pointing on one of the stone buildings in town, but he just couldn't; he was too giddy to concentrate on anything other than Mr.

Bullwhip. He decided to fish for trout downstream a little. He did this for about three hours but couldn't take it anymore. He just didn't have the patience to sit idly by and wait. He needed something completely different to think about, so he decided to go back and check on things in Fargas Union.

Making the drive into Fargas Union was as much an excuse for time to think as it was to see if there were any new eggs. Plus, he wanted one more try with Mack, to see if he could be of any help.

Harness prided himself on a life spent learning to value alternative ideas, but he had never encountered anything as complex and as full of life as what was happening now. He felt, as he never had before, the need to talk to someone else. Even if he found out nothing from Mack, at least the thought that there might be more to know would be removed.

When Harness pulled up to the Fargas Union post office, he walked past Don Barnes and Georgie Buck Able, who were, once again, at their customary sitting spot two doors down the street (in front of the hardware store where Georgie's brother, Maskin Able, worked) from the post office. Just before he walked in the post office door, Harness could make out the voices of Don and Georgie at his back.

"Looks to me like he's got a thimble in his rump, or a stitching to bring an itching," said Don Barnes.

"Got a ringer of a dinger, that's for sure, yep, a ringer of a dinger on that there headstone, Donnie," Georgie Buck Able chuckled.

"Probably flirting with the devil, swinging bullhorns and making homemade gin," Don added.

"Ouch, a bullhorn would hurt a man mighty bad, Donnie. Looks like you're right-on-the-dot again, bullhorns and gin, yep, that's what it is," added the always yacky Georgie.

Harness ignored their comments and strode straight inside to see Mack. There was no messing around for Harness right now. Two trips to town in the last week was suspicious as well. He didn't want to give any clues out.

Harness leaned over the post office counter and spotted Mack sorting through stacks of mail. "Hey, Mack?" Harness asked calmly. "Hey-ya Mack, have a moment?"

"Huh?"

"Mack? Hey, over here, it's me, Harness."

"Oh, hiya, Harness. Didn't expect to see you so soon?"

"Me, either, but sometimes things take a turn, you know. So, anything shown up?"

"Nope, nothing my friend. Looks like we've weathered that storm. It's a good thing, too. I'm hoping mostly that none of what I think happened ever really happened, to tell you the truth," answered Mack.

"If you don't mind me asking, Mack," said Harness, "now that you've had a few days to think it over. Are you positive you never heard of a Mr. Morgan Bullwhip?"

"Now, Harness, I told you no before. Not to discourage you or anything, but I don't hardly know anyone outside of Fargas Union. Never have and probably never will. I've got a small world inside this head of mine. I know you don't like it, but I've never heard of this man before." Mack paused, narrowed his eyebrows and spoke again. "Hmm, I suspect this has to do with all that supernatural stuff you brought around here the other day. I'm telling you now, and for the last time, I don't know anything and I don't want to know anything. You want small talk, feel free to come on by, but I don't want anything to do with you and this situation of yours. All you need to know is I won't spread the word. That'll have to be good enough for you." Mack might as well have stomped his feet on the ground. It felt like a boomerang had just whopped Harness on the face.

Harness knew it was over. His luck with Mack was over. From now on they had to keep their minds to themselves. He started to leave, saying, "Thanks, Mack. I'll check in more usual for awhile all the same."

"O.K. then," Mack nodded. "Now, you take care, Harness. You're looking mighty tight my friend, mighty tight."

Harness nodded good-bye, knowing full well that he was on his own now. He looked over at Georgie and Don on his way back to his truck. He straightened his neck out, tilted his lower jaw up and out as he walked. "There shall be refuge for the people I am about to hatch," thought Harness to himself. "I will be a gracious, brave and generous host." He committed himself, right then and there, to the absolute and total restoration of his new town while looking right in the deep brown irises of Don Barnes' eyes.

As Harness packed himself back in the cab of his truck, he glanced back over at Don Barnes and Georgie Buck Able. Harness thought that if they weren't the types to start spreading a story like an avalanche, he'd consider asking them if they knew anything about a Morgan Bullwhip. He knew better, though. He didn't want any troubles or ridiculous rumors stampeding around him again, like when he first moved in.

Mack walked out to watch Harness drive away. Don Barnes called Mack over with a wave of his hand and started talking. "Now tell me if I'm wrong here, Mack, but is that man not just about a lonesome hound dog with a twisted tail drawn down beneath him? Seems to me he's hoping that he'll find a wishbone to do some good luck cracking with, ain't that right there, Mack? Tell me that man's not wished upon too many stars?

Heck, a fool can spot that, even a damn fool like me can see that."

"You know, you might be right, Don. It's possible that wishbone is about to break. One thing's for sure: it won't be long before we know if Harness got the big half or the little half of his wish," replied Mack in a dreamy tone of voice.

Georgie Buck Able, who rarely missed being the first one to follow up what Don said, sat with his mouth cracked open, listening to Mack, then kicked in. "Good one, Mack. Good one. I guess ol' Don is right again. Hear that, Donnie? Even Mister Mack here agrees with you now. Ain't many times when Donnie here can't pop the top off the big ol' barrel of the unknown, ain't that right Donnie, ain't that a big ol' loud and clear 10-4?"

Don rocked a few times in his chair. He pulled a toothpick out of his pocket, stuck it in the corner of his mouth and grinned. He felt good.

Chapter Fourteen

As Harness drove back to Pick Up Stick City, he tried to piece all of the clues together. He believed that he was coming to the people of Pick Up Stick City as much as they to him. It was even possible that all of this had happened before and that he was following some inherited intuition, some mystic path.

Harness wondered again who Mr. Morgan Bullwhip was and, for that matter, how his re-birth was coming along. With that, he stepped on the accelerator and his truck lurched a little more quickly down the road.

When Harness rolled back into Pick Up Stick City, he jumped out of his truck to hustle over and see what had happened to Mr. Morgan Bullwhip. Right near the surface of the river, Harness spotted a slick, gelatin-looking hand rising and falling, splashing and flailing. A head momentarily emerged, sporting a wet coil of hair. Harness bent down quickly and, with a great tug on Mr. Bullwhip's arm, was able to pull the man onto the shore. "Greetings, Mr. Bullwhip," shouted Harness, looking into the face of Mr. Bullwhip, "Been a long time now, has it not?"

There was no answer. The clump of man Harness had pulled from the water simply moaned. Harness looked closely and saw that a thin strip of skin was still running across Morgan Bullwhip's lips and ears. He felt mean doing it, but he pushed Mr. Bullwhip back into the water, back into the smooth spin of the whirlpool where he would have to continue developing.

It wasn't long before Mr. Morgan Bullwhip rose again, and this time he responded when Harness pulled him ashore and greeted him.

"You bet the black ink of a book I'm Mr. Morgan Bullwhip. But you sure as heck aren't anyone I know," Mr. Bullwhip blurted and spewed out, shaking water from his skin.

Harness handed him an extra shirt he was wearing to dry off with and said, "Well, that's because my name's Harness Trenchold. You ended up in my mailbox, if you can believe it."

"Now if that's a fact, the mailbox and all, then I got a load of good questions to start coming your way, partner," Mr. Morgan Bullwhip said, as he slowly dried himself off. "Tell me one thing first, though. Where are the folks that jumped with me?"

"Jumped? What folks?" Harness asked, beginning to feel lost again.

"You know, the others, such as ol' Decker Tab for one thing. Or wait, he was already dried up. The lady for instance, Rubia, or Gene Rifflebutts?" Mr. Morgan Bullwhip asked.

"The others?!" Harness said. "I have other eggs like yours, but I don't really know anyone else." Harness stared at Morgan, and wild thoughts were running through his mind. Might all of this seemingly strange nonsense now begin to make sense? Mr. Bullwhip looked around a bit confused and asked, "Where's my house?"

Harness gestured with his arms vaguely in the direction of the town and asked Morgan to have a seat with him on a rock by the shore of the water. He then began explaining to Morgan how he'd learned about this town from a lady in Nebraska and that although he did believe in cloud formations and fire sculpture, he had never been fully convinced in the existence of living spirits or ghosts before, but he knew better now.

Mr. Morgan Bullwhip interrupted, "Now, wait here a goll-darn second. Do I know you? No, I don't think I do. Did you jump in the water like us, or stick it out through the sun?"

"I've always been here. I'm the only one here," Harness said.

"Well, then, where have I been? And what do you mean ghosts? I'm real, buddy boy, just as real as you'll ever be!" Mr. Bullwhip snapped.

"Yes, sir, yes, I understand. You're real alright, but you've been, well, you've been brought to life from the water just recently and living inside an egg that looked kind of like a rock until a few days ago," Harness said as politely as possible.

"Well, I know I've been in the water, Son. That's because I jumped in to hide from the sun. I thought we all did. Remember, we all tied ourselves to rocks?" Mr. Bullwhip said, his speech slowing down a bit. "I say there, do I even know you?" Morgan asked again.

"No, Morgan. No, you don't know me, but you will. The only reason I know you is because you were delivered to me in the mail, and I saw your name when I cracked you open," Harness repeated.

"Come again?" Mr. Bullwhip started in, his speech slowing down a little bit more. Harness noticed that Mr. Bullwhip had shrunk an inch or so and that a small trickle of water was leaking out of the soles of his feet. "You picked me up from a post office?" Mr. Bullwhip asked.

"That's right, but don't ask me why or how you ended up there. I've decided that you must have known all along that I would arrive," Harness replied.

"Known? I don't know anything that I can think of. You know about the sun, don't you?" asked Mr. Bullwhip.

"I don't think so, not the way you're talking about it," Harness said.

Morgan Bullwhip tilted his head a bit, looked at Harness, shook his head, then looked at the ground and began telling about the sun.

Chapter Fifteen

"Many years ago, the people who had lived here were sitting along the river that flowed out of town, tossing rocks and skipping stones, catching trout, enjoying evening picnics, in all ways living content and normal lives. There was the usual collection of folks that, well, claimed to see spaceships and the group of people that preferred money and the cleanliness that they thought currency could buy. But, on the day of the summer solstice, the healthy variety of activity in the town began to cease. A monoculture of sorts, you could say, invited itself in. This was because the sun began to take over. Shadows were destined to be melted into tar. It was to become a summer that wouldn't halt.

"People didn't really pay much notice to the shift in daylight until the beginning of August, when it became all too clear that the days had just kept getting longer and longer—even though the summer solstice had come and gone. Decker Tab, who was the mayor back then, told his neighbor Neil Flinch, the newspaper publisher, that it would be best if the paper didn't start making the increase in sunlight an issue just yet. He didn't want people in other cities wondering what was wrong with this town. It would be best to lock the story in and take care of the problem without any outside fuss. If I know those two, which I do, their conversation probably went something like this:

"'Well Decker, here's the deal anyway. The sun won't bargain much, I reckon. It is what it is, not what we hope. So, whether we talk or not, it's not likely to wince.

Plus, I don't see that it makes much difference. It's not like anybody would believe us anyway. Facts or no facts, you know what I'm getting at? We're stuck any way we go. If I ran the story, we'd be laughed at. On the flip side, if people find out we didn't tell anyone, we'll still be laughed at,' Neil Flinch explained.

"'I know, I know, I know, Neil. You understand just like me, we're caught. Let's not tell anyone, I say. After all, it's the principle. We have to work alone as long as we can.' Then Decker added, 'It's a matter of pride is what it is, you understand, proud and proper, prudent people,' Decker said. Neil Flinch nodded in agreement. For now, no story would be published.

"People only got nervous, though, not telling anyone else," Morgan continued. "By the time November rolled around, not only had the days become slowly and slowly longer, but brighter as well. The incredible halogen daytime light wasn't cooperating with the sleeping habits of people. Nearly everyone in town had been raised to work hard all day and sleep at night, but it was rare when a person was able to grab much more than a couple hours of sleep in November. Now that all they had was brighter and brighter days, night only lasted about four hours or so. In December it was worse, twenty-two hours of sun. By the end of February, what everyone used to know as nighttime had been gone for over a week. Even the shadows were worn out.

"Sheri Louis, a little third grade girl, squealed one morning when she watched her shadow creep away from her and hide under a rock. It was weird, everyone agreed, not to have a shadow anymore. Yet Decker Tab, who had not slept for nearly a month and a half, still wouldn't talk to the neighboring towns. Now it wasn't because he was too embarrassed to tell the truth, but because he was so sunburnt and in such a manic state of mind that he doubted anyone would pay much attention to anything he had to say.

"By the middle of April, people were just plain, plumb, dopey crazy. They were trading fingerprints, laughing hysterically at their friends for no reason, making cow noises, even setting a place at the dinner table for the sun. Things were getting to the point where it was rare when three to four people could sit together and carry on a civilized conversation, since everyone was either angry or scared, not to mention confused.

"Ms. Viola Green had become so upset with the sun that she had looked right at it, hands on her hips, and given it a piece of her mind. She yelled so long that when she looked away from the sun, her eyes just caught on fire. Nothing, not even crying, could save her eyesight. Absolutely nothing. All through her wailing and screaming and cussing, the sun kept shining. But, perhaps as a small consolation for Ms. Green, the sun did stop being something she could see.

"Nate Copple hid no feelings about how he felt, either. 'My sweat glands, I tell you, are all used up. If not for my spit, I'd have no way to cool down. Damn sun has gone run amuck from gravity! The end of the world is coming!'

"The sun seemed to be playing mean tricks on everyone. Laurel Smitterson, Junior High Student Class President, told her mother she wanted to be a sun when she grew up. Gene Rifflebutts came up with an idea to reinvent the sunflower. People had begun to talk of nighttime and shadows as if they were things they used to have to walk twenty miles, uphill, to see back in the old days." Morgan Bullwhip paused as though he needed to catch his breath or gather his thoughts. He then resumed his story.

"It was about a year later when things began to take another drastic change. This was when the first person, Tullet Bloodsuck, dried up completely and shrank into a small piece of parched skin. Decker Tab had been called over to see Tullet and, in response, suggested that they roll him up and stick him in a bottle for safekeeping. Neil Flinch added that they should tie Tullet up in the bottle to a rope and let him float in the river.

"Over the next few weeks more than half the women, men and children had been rolled up and stuck into bottles, jars, boxes, all labeled as to who they were. Some of the people still alive—myself, Lucas Stunt, Patti Grinbelt and Gene Rifflebutts—thought that the remaining people in town ought to tie themselves to rocks and just jump into what little water still remained beneath the waterfall. Decker Tab was absolutely against this. He suggested that everyone pitch together and fight like men, maybe make a giant quilt to hang over the town, do anything for shade. Gene Rifflebutts told Decker there was no point, that either decision was suicide.

"Everyone looked at Decker Tab for a response, but he had dried up on the spot and turned to parchment. 'Seal him up,' said Gene Rifflebutts and Neil Flinch at the same time.

"'All in all, I'd say old Decker was a good mayor. Heck, this sun thing would drive any mayor crazy,' Lucas Stunt had proclaimed as he stuffed Decker inside an old bottle, tossing him into the river.

"After sealing up Decker, the rest of the people in town tied rocks to their arms, legs, necks and stomachs, wrote their names on pieces of paper, stuck their nametags in their mouths and jumped into the pool of water beneath the waterfall.

"I suppose it must have been sometime later that the sun started setting again. But, of course, we never knew it. Out of the blue, exempt from history, the whole town just disappeared without a trace.

"Well, that's the whole shebang, my friend. That's all there is to know. That sun was our blessing, then our fate and then our disaster," Mr. Morgan Bullwhip uttered in a stoic manner.

Harness had sat mute while Morgan spoke about the sun, and there was a good five minutes of silence when he was done speaking. The wind picked up and the sun went behind a cloud. Then Morgan spoke again, almost to himself. "I wonder if maybe this spot isn't the center of a flat earth, and so, like an equator, we hadn't been able to swerve away from the sun that year?"

Morgan could barely speak by this time. He had needed to be soaked in the water to be brought back to life, and now he was drying up, shrinking before Harness' very eyes. He was losing energy, needing to breathe deeply between sentences.

"Who else can I expect to hatch? Who else jumped with you?" Harness asked. Mr. Bullwhip didn't answer. Again Harness asked, "Mr. Bullwhip? Morgan, who can I expect to hatch?" Unfortunately, Morgan was so tired and small at this point, he was only able to grunt, like a fish out of water.

Right before drying out completely, Morgan mustered one last gurgle of words. He sputtered, "It's not just us that will change you, Harness. It's the land all around here, the fields, the water, this valley. They are more than just space. This land is full of surprises. Memories are alive here. Be patient, Harness." Having uttered this, Morgan Bullwhip's mouth molded shut and his ears closed up. Within a few moments he had returned to the shape of an egg.

Harness picked him up and carried him to where he stored the other eggs, in an old outhouse not more than twenty feet from the river's edge. He wondered to himself what he was going to do with his new power of creation. He had never been an overly zealous or religious man, but he suddenly felt a bit uncomfortable. Now, somewhat capable of creation, he feared he had been given too much power, something reserved for the gods. He would have to be careful, but he figured there was some reason why he had been placed in this position.

Chapter Sixteen

Over the course of a few weeks, Harness slowly and surely brought each person back to life, and with each new person came new information, new stories, new conversations. For instance, Harness discovered that Mr. Gene Rifflebutts and Louis Fermister had extensive knowledge of carpentry as well as practical advice on restoring stone walls. When Harness began foundation work on the old pharmacy, he merely hatched the two of them, and they helped him out with useful advice along the way.

Most "births" were successful. Not all, though. One of the worst had been Gordon Goodgrin, who exclaimed Harness was totally invading his privacy. "I've been perfectly satisfied not to be among the living a long time now, son. Who gave you the permission to bring me back? Do you want to know something about privacy? I'll tell you about privacy."

Thus began a memorable story by Mr. Goodgrin.

Chapter Seventeen

"I'll tell you one thing for certain, son, it's no fun at all to have barbed wire for a backbone, and that's what I had for three nights and two days. Plus, I had my father's stare on me for a week. You see, people aren't meant to be seen the way they really are. Being social is a choice people make. What gives another person a chance to be free shouldn't be taken advantage of. It feels rotten to do what I wouldn't want done to me.

"Aunt Joist told me right away that I shouldn't have done what I did and that I would find disasters falling from my shoulders longer than water flowed downhill. She ended up being right in a way, plus, I got scared, real scared, for awhile.

"It wasn't really anything to me at the time. I'd just looked in Ms. Fleecee Rejoy's window one night and saw her drinking beneath a bare-watted light bulb. All she'd been wearing was an old bathrobe all colored with tiny gray dots. She also had plastic bags held to her feet with rubber bands around the tops of her ankles. I hardly noticed her face the way it blended in so well with the gray dots on her bathrobe. The room she was in had a candle burning steady beneath a pale-colored painting of an ocean wave and a single plant (looked like a dandelion to me) growing out of a white foam cup. The room was like a broken clock, as if time had been worn out and now stood still, a place where recorded music skipped over and over again. The room wasn't so much pathetic as it was drab and mundane. It was the kind of place reserved for muttering, puttering, stuttering in.

"The reason I looked in the first place was because of the voice I heard. I was walking by her place one night when I was positive I heard some lady whispering to me. I even remember saying out loud, 'What? Huh? Who's there? What's that?' I can't say I heard anyone answer back, but I wouldn't swear I didn't hear anyone answer back, either.

"Looking around, I was soon being guided by a light shining through the trees coming from Ms. Rejoy's house. I went twenty yards, maybe, and that's when she became visible through the screen of her back porch. She was walking, kind of staggering, really, back and forth with a tumbler full of clear homemade moonshine in her hand and shouting slurred salutes of celebration on behalf of random things around her. Hailing the beauty of her indoor flower garden, the trees in her yard, the ocean wave, the sturdy floorboards, anything she could see. She would begin each celebration with her arm raised well up above her head and concluded each outburst with the line, 'For the love of Judas Priest, this one's for the holiest spirit!' I must have heard her say this thirty times. It was like she had a magic wand in her grip, she seemed so attached and competent with that glass in her hand. Over and over she muttered strings of words then—PRESTO—a loud declaration would be made, the obligatory toast hoisted in honor of the moment, then down would go another drink, slurping quickly past her throat. Of course, I had never seen an old woman drink before, let alone seen an old woman drunk, so not watching was completely out of the question. I stared hard. I hate to admit it, but I stared a long hard time until Ms. Rejoy fell asleep, all slouched up ragged against the wall of her porch.

"The only other experience I'd had with drunk people was something my friend Chip Tweed once told me about the Bloan sisters who lived nearby to him. Chip said that the Bloan sisters used to make what he called mexicali near his house in the apple orchard. He got to see them because they were his neighbors, and they never tried to hide from anyone's sight. Even though they were Chip's neighbors and pretty obvious ones at that, Chip's dad, Palamino Tweed, would never admit to noticing them. When he did admit their existence, he'd profess it in an opposite and negative way. 'We ain't got no neighbors, unless you count them two creatures living a mile away from here. Them two ought to be shot, filled with lard, ground to burger at best.' Chip's dad had a quick way of seeing things and a temper to go along with it. Anyway, mexicali was Chip's word for explaining a person being drunk and having a good time all at once. Chip said that when he saw the Bloan sisters doing what he called mexicali, it looked like a couple of people in love on a roller coaster. He said they would lie on the ground, point to the sky, push each other over, eat grass, peel bark off the apple trees and eat it—all sorts of things—and no matter what they did, they would laugh and giggle and cry.

"Chip said, 'They'd start laughing so hard it's not even funny. They'd act like a couple of people discovering laughter for the first time.' Chip added that, in his opinion, when the Bloan sisters got to laughing, they seemed kind of scared about being happy.

"I told Chip that, to me, mexicali didn't sound like too much fun if it was like being scared. It seemed more like being sad.

"Chip answered, 'Sure, maybe, but as far as I care the Bloan sisters are just a couple of drunks who are fun to watch.'

"As far as I could tell from the night I watched Ms. Rejoy drinking, she wasn't involved in any sort of mexicali. She didn't seem to be laughing at all. She seemed a long and far ways off, mostly lost, some angry, partly searching for relief. It was as if her mind had been tied up and twisted behind her back. Once, when she held her drinking glass up to her lips, she'd missed the rim of the glass and bit down too hard, piercing her lips together so tight that it made her face turn red, causing her lower lip to bleed. When she did this, the glare on her face took on such a look of meanness that it was possible to imagine bullets erupting out of her eye sockets.

"Right before she fell asleep the night I watched, I saw her act real mean. I saw her spit hard, like a sneezing bull, into the screen that I was watching her through. I was startled because I got the feeling she'd noticed I was watching. Seeing this put what felt like a big hard knot into my neck. I starting feeling embarrassed and scared all at once. I wondered what Chip would call having these two feelings together. I knew I wasn't supposed to have been watching and that if Ms. Rejoy had wanted a guest, she would have invited me over. I felt dirty. By the time I got home I was too afraid to go to sleep since I was certain I'd be lying down to a series of bad nightmares. Not only that, I believed I deserved nightmares. There's no way I had heard any voices calling me to watch Ms. Rejoy. Why would there have been?

"Probably because I'm stupid I went back. The next evening I watched Ms. Rejoy again. I saw her walking around in her yard this time. She was drinking and declaring toasts to the world around her.

"As I watched her move along, toasting the wide open world in the late evening light, I was amazed at how old she was. She was hunched so low to the ground she could have used a handle on her neck and a partner to hold her face up out of the dirt. Ms. Rejoy came across as a

76

heaping mountain of ancient age. It seemed everything over her ankles was above tree line. I decided this lady I was spying on seemed mostly unreal. She lived so close to the earth she was practically buried.

"Then, a peculiar thing happened. Stopping every few steps, she would meow, calling for cats to come and see her. Passionately, she would drape her hands out. Whispering hands. Hands which seemed to melt in the air, hands that seem to be dripping with milk. Her hands would sneak out and touch the fur of kittens who had magically begun to surround her after she called them.

"It seemed as though a certain pleasure overtook Ms. Rejoy. It was like the cat fur and her hands were able to charm one another. After stroking the kittens for awhile, I noticed her legs moving like ocean waves. That's when I turned around and walked off. I knew it was bad watching once, but it was pitiful watching this lady a second time. Again, I felt an ache spreading down my neck, through my back. I felt stiff and sad. It was obvious to me at that moment that people deserved to be left alone, not seen or spied on. My heart was about to blow up. My face felt bright red and overheated. Getting home, I kept tripping over my feet because I was looking over my shoulder so often. I was certain something was following me.

"Then the real hard parts came along.

"The next afternoon I asked my mom if she knew anything about Ms. Rejoy, and it just so happened that my Aunt Joist was there, too. They usually got together in our kitchen during the afternoons to make bread and rolls. Now to tell the truth, I was pretty certain that my mom didn't know much about Ms. Rejoy, but I believed Aunt Joist would. I figured, as well, that whatever Aunt Joist knew would be exaggerated since she was a bit of a gossip and tended to make mountains out of molehills. All the same though, I wanted to know more.

"'What do you want to know?' my mom asked back without any suspicion.

"'What I'd like to know is what you want to know for?' Aunt Joist blurted in. 'That lady ain't nothing more than a chigger 'neath a person's skin. Just thinking of her makes me itch.'

"'There's not much to know,' my mom said. 'She tends to herself and invites no one into her business.'

"Aunt Joist said, 'Well, that's just the half of it! She's looking for revenge is what I've heard. Why, the last time I said anything to that lady was following the funeral of her husband. Everyone knows she killed him just so she could live alone. But before that, a few years before you were born, son, she got so drunk she turned into a barrel of whiskey, lit a match and turned to fire. Then she had the gall to let her tongue burn like a wick for days while she laid, flat on her back, on her front lawn. If it were possible for a person to be a ghost, then Ms. Rejoy would be a likely candidate to prove it.'

"'So, she's crazy,' I said.

"'Crazy?! Ha, crazy's too nice a word. She's the root, the core, the meaning, the center source of all that's mean and evil. If I were you I wouldn't even look at her. If anyone could read your mind, chase you down in the dead of night, haunt your dreams, give you bad luck, it would be Ms. Rejoy. It's for certain that she hates people and will do anything to prove it.' Aunt Joist rambled on just like I thought she would. Unfortunately, I knew Aunt Joist wasn't too far off from what other people thought about Ms. Rejoy, since my mom wasn't interrupting anything she said.

"'How would you know if she was trying to haunt you?' I asked.

"'You'd be silent and pale just about everywhere you went. She would suck the life right out of you. You'd turn into a mud puddle, or a stack of dead bird feathers.

I declare, if anyone could kill that lady it would be a blessing for all of us. It's just not healthy having a dead soul like her living amongst us. Not healthy at all.'

"'Why doesn't someone kill her, then?' I asked.

"'Okay, okay, that's enough!' my mom declared. 'Let's not get carried away now, Joist. No one's going to kill anyone. That's ridiculous.'

"Not listening, Aunt Joist kept on talking. 'Why doesn't someone kill her, you ask? Well, I'll tell you why. It's impossible to hit a moving target that can read minds and has eyes in the back of her head. Plus, that lady gets in people's dreams before they can surprise attack her.'

"'Aunt Joist! That's enough now!' my mom said.

"I'm not sure why I said it, but I did. 'I could kill her easy. I know when she gets drunk and seems sad. I know because I've been watching her.'

"Well, that put the room into a panic, into a spinning, airborne, stilled-motion gasp. I felt more dead than alive, like my tongue was the flavor of cold, dull brass. My mom just stood and looked at me, then put her flour-covered hands to her face and inhaled sharply. When she pulled her hands back down, she looked all white. Aunt Joist started wiping her nose with a dish rag, back and forth, a little quicker each wipe. She was sweating. Then she said, 'Tell me what you saw. Tell me what it was, son. Tell me, what did you see?'

"I told Aunt Joist and Mom how I had seen Ms. Rejoy drinking and about her petting the kittens. Then Aunt Joist said that I'd messed up real big and that disasters would tumble down my shoulders longer than water flowed downhill. Both my mom and Aunt Joist seem visibly shaken, worried and upset.

"Even though it never made sense to me, I was sent to my room that night as a punishment. I guess I was supposed to think about what I'd done on an empty stomach. At least that's what I ended up doing. While I lay on my bed, staring up at my walls, I wondered why it had been so easy for me to spy on a person who was supposedly supernatural. I decided that I must have some sort of supernatural power, too, or that I sure was lucky when it came to knowing supernatural things. After awhile my mind changed a little. I remembered again how terrible I felt each time I'd watched Ms. Rejoy. I remembered how hot and red my face got. I also began wondering why my back was beginning to feel tense and coiled up.

"It was the next day when I surprised myself by pulling a handful of metal filings from my back pocket. Later, during that same day, I reached in my pocket to show Chip the metal filings, but out came a handful of roofing nails instead. Chip thought it was kind of funny that I was carrying a pocketful of roofing nails around with me. I thought it was weird that the filings had swelled to nails. Next, Chip gawked at me kind of funny and asked, 'Is that a strand of wire sticking out of your shirt?'

"'Huh?'" I said.

"Chip looked behind my neck and hollered, 'Yeah, it is. It is wire. Hey, you got barbed wire in your back!' He began laughing, pointing at me like I was a joke. I turned pale as soggy white bread and took off running toward home.

"While I was running, I broke down and started sobbing like a baby. I could feel the barbed wire in my back, and it was growing and twisting up like a tornado. I hoped my dad or mom could come up with a miracle to cure me.

"When I finally got home, it wasn't like I'd reached a paradise. I was trembling and short of breath. To boot, while Aunt Joist had been helping my mom do the laundry, a bottle of clear-colored moonshine whiskey like Ms. Rejoy had been drinking had fallen out of the pocket of my jeans. As I walked up the steps of our front porch, my mom, Aunt Joist and my dad were all waiting for me silently. When I saw the three of them standing before me like a cast iron fence, I knew I was going to find out a few more reasons why I shouldn't have been watching Ms. Rejoy.

"'A-hem,' my dad cleared his throat. 'Got yourself a drinking problem?' he asked.

"'Not much point in asking that,' started Aunt Joist. 'The boy's got that kind of problem and a whole lot more. It won't matter what he tells you.'

"'No.' I said.

"'Then what are you doing carrying a bottle around with you for? Maybe this'll explain your stories about seeing Ms. Rejoy,' my dad stated.

"'But Dad, I got hurt. I got a strand of barbed wire growing out of me!' I twisted and turned to try and show them the wire. I was crying again. 'I don't have a bottle of nothing anywhere, plus I know I've been doing what I shouldn't be doing. I've been butting into Ms. Rejoy's life and I know I shouldn't have been but...'

"Aunt Joist interrupted, 'You sure shouldn't have been, that's for certain, and now I bet that old lady is going to torture you until the last sunset you see...'

"Dad held up his arms, sucked in his lips and blew out a loud blast of air from his mouth, silencing Aunt Joist, 'QUIET JOIST! QUIET! Just hold your mouth, would you!? You have what coming out of you, son?'

"Barbed wire," I whispered, looking down to my toes, waiting. But no one said anything. I just stood silently, expecting them to think I had become a drunk. Instead, I heard everyone gasp; they could see the twisting coils of barbed wire coming out of me.

"After a few minutes of staring, we all went inside and I stood there, watching them all talk about wire, fences, Ms. Rejoy, morals, listening to my teachers and how I'd better start going to church. Everyone agreed, there probably wasn't an easy cure for what I had done. This was going to be a problem that took time to solve. I wasn't used to my parents showing any emotion. Usually they talked when I wasn't in the room, but this had been too much. They weren't taking this in what seemed to be their usual calm manner. I believe now what caused them so much grief was fear and the fact that this wouldn't be something they could tackle and overcome immediately as they, and I, were used to.

"Later on that evening, when I would usually be going off to bed, my dad directed me to his study and started giving me a lecture. He didn't seem all that angry, but mostly serious. He seemed taken away with a notion of some kind. 'Son, you probably don't know what it's like to be alive, do you? I would guess you don't even believe in life.'

"'What do you mean, sir?' I said.

Dad looked at me with an empty stare, paused, then started to speak again. It was obvious I wasn't supposed to say anything.

"'When a person closes their door, they want to be alone. People need to know they can do this and be free. It's a way of being able to breathe easy, to rest as fresh snow on a sunny day, to have the chance to do some dreaming, to wish and wonder and believe that you are more, could have been more, will be more than you have been in your life so far. Regret seeps in, and there is an echo of sadness that fills you, makes you wish for the memory, the zest, the energy of childhood. You will never be all you've hoped and dreamed of, but, in private, in a silent reverie, at least you can pretend...' Dad stopped and looked like he was beginning to cry, which seemed incredible to me.

"I sat numbly, listening to silence. I knew he was thinking hard, trying very hard to get a point across to me, to tell me something important. He took another deep breath. The light above us started buzzing. The air seemed coarse like wet sandpaper. I itched my face and felt sore. He began again. 'People are delicate, like eggs and mist. It's important to know that everyone's not the same. Most of what comes across as ugly is really just self-defense.'

"'Yes sir,' I said.

I could tell that Dad was still talking to himself more than to me. He didn't seem completely aware that I was even in front of him. He kept on. 'Growing old is private. No one wants to admit mistakes they've made or want others to know the things they lust after, still quest for. Simple things become invisible, and complications get more complicated. You look at pictures of yourself when you were four, maybe seven, thirteen years old and spend hours wondering who it was that you were back then, wondering where you've gone to, wondering where did life go? You recall the good luck given to you by your aunts and uncles. You feel ashamed.' He stalled, wet his lips, and seemed pale and soft and sad. My dad seemed like some stranger I had never met before.

"'Yes sir.' I said again.

"Then, suddenly, his shoulders hunched up a little bit. He sat back up in his chair and was speaking like his old self again. 'Son, folks carry secrets inside them that make their lives worth living. It is a slow and careful way of being. Everyone has an imagination. You have your own thoughts and wishes you don't want anyone to know, don't you?'

"'Yes,' I said.

"'What do you need to do now? I'm not certain, really, but I do know this: If you can't make yourself enjoy life on your own, you're no more than a problem. Real life isn't like television; people aren't asking you to watch them.' Dad raised his arms and stood up, motioned for me to leave the room.

"I got up and left quietly after this.

"When I got back to my room and laid down to go to sleep, I think I finally understood what had happened. People had lives which weren't supposed to be seen and that being sorry didn't mean a whole lot unless you meant it.

"The barbed wire in my back kept me from being able to move or sleep very well another three days. It was sharp and rusty. It took at least two days before I felt the first section loosen up. On the third night I was able to reach behind my back and peel off the barbed wire like a snake skin. I was able to stand up and not ache with pain. I suddenly felt okay, just a little stiff.

"When Aunt Joist saw me walking into the kitchen the next morning, she looked surprised, but relieved as well. 'Looks like you may have some luck after all. If you can survive this, you'll have the Lord on your side until the sun decides to burn out.'

"I told her I had a job to do and left the kitchen.

"What I came up with to do was pretty easy, but then again, my problem started out easily, too. The solution made perfect sense to me. Of course, without the three days of barbed wire in my back, I never would have come up with what I did.

"What happened is that I placed a big bowl of warm cream and two kittens at Ms. Rejoy's front door. I walked away on my tiptoes and never saw Ms. Rejoy again in my life. I wanted to give her something that would take her mind away from me but that would also show I cared. Something that showed I was giving back what I felt I'd taken away.

"The reason I believe I was forgiven was because the next day, while playing with Chip, I reached into my pants pocket for a pocket knife and pulled out a few rays of sunlight instead. At the same moment that I held the sunshine in my hand, I had the urge to straighten out my back and stand real tall again. When I stood up straight, it felt like a bowl of warm whipping cream was poured down my spine." And with that, Mr. Goodgrin ended his story.

After a few moments he added, "Don't bring me back again, Mr. Harness. I can't speak for anyone else, I know, but don't bring me back again unless I ask."

Harness was just about to ask, "How will I know when you ask?" but Gordon Goodgrin was all dried up.

Chapter Eighteen

Mr. Goodgrin aside, most people didn't mind being brought to life at all; they were just surprised. Mr. Rifflebutts and Louis Fermister, for instance, enjoyed sitting around and telling Harness about their lives while he worked. The two of them both agreed it never crossed either of their minds that their town would ever die out. Being human, though, each felt there must have been some reason for what happened.

One day Harness suggested, "Maybe burning up your old town was like setting fire to the prairie? Maybe burning the town has improved the roots and will allow for a better life here?"

Both men nodded. Gene Rifflebutts added, "Maybe so, Harness. Maybe you're right. I mean, I have become somewhat immortal, haven't I?" Mr. Rifflebutts looked at Louis when he said this and they grinned. "Immortal. That has a certain musical pitch to it, doesn't it?"

Most of their conversations, though, were reminiscent. One day Mr. Rifflebutts asked, "Just why was it that our kids always left this place? It wasn't really such a bad spot was it?"

Mr. Fermister responded, "I couldn't say exactly, but I do know they always wanted to get out of here bad. I'm sure this place seemed pretty small and boring. I suppose we adults spent too much time talking about cities as being the real world or something, even though I don't believe that now.

"All the same, though, it was pretty sad to watch our kids just up and leave all the time. Honestly, watching them all leave made me feel like a failure. My own son, Lomax, left, but he didn't become the big shot he thought he deserved to be off in the Twin Cities, that's for sure. As far as I could tell, he just worked long hours for low pay at some marketing company. He could have been his own boss with a real good business right here in town, but he thought he was going to be better than that. I remember having to keep my mouth shut when he told me about his life. It always sounded like he was being taken advantage of."

"I suppose it's much the same as my daughter and son. Each went off to be in California. They were obsessed with the new frontiers of the Pacific Ocean. I never understood any of it, honestly," said Mr. Rifflebutts.

The conversation wasn't that much different from many Harness listened to. The two men would wile away the time, talking about this and that, until each dried back up.

There was no end to the pleasure Harness derived from hearing people discuss the past. One of the stories Harness liked best was told to him by a man named Henry Harsh.

Over the course of an entire day, Henry told Harness about the old town fairs, how they always had pie and ice cream contests, the most unusual cooked dish contest, the most inventive gelatin dessert, as well as a rather drab but well-attended parade featuring the Prairie Wind Queen and her Royal Gamma Grass Court. Henry also told Harness about the Spiral Ring.

"The Spiral Ring was an annual ritual the whole town attended," Henry began. "Everyone would leave their houses, come together and sit in a series of loops, outward in a spiral. From above, the whole town would have looked like a hurricane, I imagine.

"The ritual was based on everyone sharing stories that expanded upon what was said the year before." He paused, "You see what I'm getting at, don't you, Harness? You understand, right? That's why it was called a Spiral Ring and not a circle game, or box play, or something." Just to be sure his point was made, Henry added, "It was not a circle. We didn't go over the same things year after year like a lot of towns and groups do, bickering over problems and things that never change."

When Harness didn't say anything to interrupt, Henry started speaking again. "Our whirling of stories wasn't a detail, or a game either. We learned about each other, exposed ourselves without regard for fear. Thinking about it now, it sure was something when we all sat and shared like that. It truly was something."

"How did it work? What did you do?" Harness asked, curious about the specifics.

"Well, the rules, if you could call them rules, were that the men and women of town would speak about the following four things." And he began counting off on his fingers.

"One, something they had done during the past year which they were proud of.

"Two, recall a memory they'd had about someone who had died during their lives.

"Three, reveal something personal to each person in their family who still lived in town.

"Four, a person would answer any questions asked of them the year before and then ask up to two questions they wanted answers to the following year.

"This would all take place out loud, starting in mid-afternoon and continue on into the evening, after the ice cream contest had settled in folks' stomachs.

"Even though it was a rather long event, I don't remember the children ever being rowdy or restless. Even the dogs seemed to hush down, and many times the river seemed to become still. Everyone would take what was said into deep consideration. For many, the Spiral Ring was the only time they ever saw men genuinely laughing or crying. People were most alive in the ring.

"For many, the Spiral Ring was something they waited for with mixed emotion. Oftentimes with a sense of nervous dread. Yet there was no event more honored or trusted. Everyone understood there was no better way to unveil themselves, to jostle demons and release dreams from their heads.

"The catch, of course, was that you could only speak in the spiral once each year. When someone said something about you, or asked you anything, it was forbidden to answer or respond until the following year. Only getting answers and asking questions once a year meant you needed to be careful with what you said and how you asked. For instance, no one could get married any sooner than one year's time since you had to ask for the hand of a partner, then wait one year to hear the answer. Although impossible to enforce, it was also strictly forbidden to leak any clues or ideas early. Most seemed to adhere to the unwritten rule of silence since surprises were fairly continual during each year's spiral." Henry tried to remember what age young people joined the discussion. He thought it had been seventeen.

Harness asked how there was time for everyone to speak, and Henry explained that the town was never much bigger than eighty people and that over half the town was less than sixteen years old. "The last year there couldn't have been much more than twenty-five. Most people didn't talk more than fifteen, twenty minutes tops," he said.

"This is remarkable, Henry. Do you recall what you told everyone during your last spiral?"

"Funny you should ask, Harness. I doubt I'll ever forget my last one. That was a doozy, really a memorable one. I remember it almost too well."

CHAPTER NINETEEN

"I lost my wife, as you all know, last year. Not to death, but to open space. She left me for a trailer nestled in the woods of Northern California, some place in the Alps of Trinity, I believe. She left me here with her momma's anger. Most of you probably thought I'd die without Louise around me this past year. I agree, I thought so, too. She was a mighty piece of strength for me and my daughter, but since she left, I can't believe the way I used to be.

"Living with her and our anger and petty outbursts and tempers and spending habits. I tell you, we scrutinized each other so closely, so afraid to let the each other be who they wanted to be, both of us loaded full shot of jealousy and insecurity. Loopy rings of misunderstanding ruled our lives. I wanted to be happy and she wanted to be happy. But I wanted to be happy first, or wanted her happy for me, and I wanted her happy my way and she her way and so on.

"There was compassion, and I did believe we were in love back then, but now I believe they were unwelcome efforts to get favors and sympathy, just misdirected attempts to break me and set herself free. Those days I used to worry about such small things, about dishes being stacked in a cupboard all neat and straight, about whether I got home by three, not three o ten. How upset I'd get if dinner wasn't ready for me. How food had to be what I liked, when I wanted it, without any changes or differences. No doubt, I drove my family crazy with all the pestering and bad manners. We were all so tense and angry it's embarrassing now. I'm just surprised that I didn't become the tail of a skunk and blow up, the way I must have smelled to all of them. Sometimes it was even worse. I would pretend I didn't care. I'd just tell my wife, my daughter, to do what they wanted, 'just go be happy,' I'd say. 'Do whatever you please.' This was worse somehow. It was like they couldn't do anything then, or if they did do something and started enjoying themselves, I'd look over, all filled up with a grudge, and pester them no end. How so? Not acknowledging accomplishment but claiming it's no big deal. If my daughter had invented God, I would have said, 'Yeah, I knew you could, no biggie. Would you start doing something to really impress me sometime?' Heck, if they'd have built the Golden Gate Bridge out of scrap metal, I'd have just said, 'Oh, okay, great, what's the big deal?'"

"I don't blame Louise for leaving. We'd never have agreed. I have spent a lot of time sitting in my backyard or at the tavern trying to figure out what took over me during my life of marriage, all thirty-four years of it. I've taken up hiking lately, to get out in the world, and have been thinking about life in terms of nature and the seasons and the cycles and the pace of breezes and animals. I've been looking for mushrooms. Been thinking how slowness needs to become part of life, not speed. I've come to think life is too short to go fast. If water can overcome mountains, then surely patience can overcome my mistakes.

"I've been wondering how I became who I am, and it seems it has mostly come about by mistake. If I had stuck with my goals and shared them with my wife, it would have, might have, worked out. Then again, nothing in my early life seems to suggest what I've become. I was the happiest, most smiling kid in the world. Full of adventure and curiosity. I was even brave. I was rarely angry and really did care about other people. Over time

I turned the opposite. I can't say I know of any single mistake I made along the way to alter. If someone asked me what changed me, I'd probably say greed, just a small slip into the desire for money and fame. You take a step in the wrong direction, even for one moment, it opens up a whole new trail. You can't go completely back and maybe that's what I've been waiting for: the moment in the past to return when I could go down the other path. I just don't know.

"I think I just walked backwards more than anything, acted like I didn't care about anything for so long, got led so far astray, that without knowing it, I put myself into a corner, and when Louise finally up and left I realized I ought to become concerned. Now, of course, I understand I waited too long, that I had turned into such a narrow way, become stuck so far from what I cared about that I'd turned into a hungry animal, feisty and dangerous, locked in a tiny caged-up, personal world. I couldn't—well, wouldn't, to be more precise—admit this. Today, I want to say I'm sorry to myself more than anything. And I bet Louise is probably the happiest woman in the world, getting away from me and turning into what she always wanted to.

"I wish I could think of things that would bring us together again before we are dead and full of wishes."

Henry paused and took a deep breath before continuing, looking off into space.

"And to answer your question from last year, Louise, even though you are not here anymore, yes, I loved you, yes I hated you, but most of all, I am sorry that I grabbed on to you and stole what you had to offer. I took the things I liked about you and used them up. Your creativity, your smile, your cooking and your wishes to be spontaneous. I now know they were only fears I had. I picked you dry. I killed you. I took for myself and spread it too far, tried to mold everything to fit me. I hope you will find calm water and perfect tomato plants in your new world. I hope you run smooth and become what I most liked about you: free and alive. Louise, I love you, and I'm sorry, so very sorry."

At this point, even though he was retelling his story, Henry had tears streaming down his face. "And, finally, I ask of my daughter, what can I teach you? Tell me it's not too late for me to teach you at least one good thing about this world. Please."

Henry stopped talking and sat quietly. "Oh my, I didn't expect this to be so realistic, Harness. These revelations sure brought me back," he said whispering. "Sharing my life in such honest terms allowed me to shed my regrets and pain. I felt clean again, changed, before the sun had so suddenly dried us all up. The weights from my heart had been released. I felt taller and bolder and more alive."

Harness mulled over everything Henry had told him. Churning questions around in a person's head for a year seemed to make for answers and recollections that were painfully accurate and heartfelt and, as a result, people asked questions that they really wanted answered. What Harness saw for the first time was that the advantages of a small town often can't be seen when you simply pass through in a car, that a small community can have deep, original concerns which bind people together for life.

The southern drizzle they'd been sitting in eventually ended, and Henry ever so quietly dried up, at which point Harness put Henry in his pocket and carried him back to the box and placed him carefully with the others.

Chapter Twenty

One day, when Mrs. Flannery Hutthutt was hatched by Harness, she mentioned the Spiral Rings as well, but not right off. Mrs. Hutthutt seemed a little bit loony, and she took to telling Harness about a time when, attached to the rock under the water, she had dreamt about a thing called microwaves and then ended up with burned fingertips. She also said she'd had a vision about the future, about the coming of the new millennium: she foresaw a different kind of flood, a different sort of second coming of Noah. She foresaw a sickeningly slow and solid flood of gravel, asphalt and cement across the land. She was concerned about the animals and the birds, the plants and the people. Without anything but hard surfaces over the earth, how would things breathe, eat, or live?

Mrs. Hutthutt also told Harness about how people used to eat hefty meals in the old days, but in the middle of the day, not at the end, so they didn't gain weight but made use of the calories; how there was no such thing as "the news" in the old days, just memories, stories and hopeful chatter. And the word "visit" used to mean sitting with a friend for a few hours, catching up with your small talk in a slow and comfortable fashion.

"We probably learned more about each other from how we talked than what we said. As for weather reports, well, that took the cake!" She told Harness how she had laughed so hard one day when she went to see her sister in Maryland and heard a man telling what the weather was going to be on the new machine everyone called a radio. She'd looked at her sister and declared, "Why, sister, what has this world come to that a person can't look out their window and tell what the weather's bringing? You can't do a thing about a rainstorm anyhow. My-o-my the things we have come to think of as making up our life."

In the end, after telling Harness a variety of things, of recollections, it was the Spiral Ring that Mrs. Hutthutt landed on. She explained it as such a flamboyant and dazzling, meaningful event; how it celebrated persistence and well-thought-out expression. "It was a method of keeping track of time," she explained to Harness. "Each Spiral Ring meant things had changed and survived. With my memory I could look back on the years by recalling the stories I'd heard. For instance, the year Frank Featherwell had told about a thorn being driven through the palm of his hand, that's easy. That's also the year I moved to a new house. Or the year Ms. April Longshadow discovered she could hatch butterflies in her sunflower garden, that's easy, too. That's the year the bank burned down. Of course there was the year that Aldo Hash finished siding his house with metal beer cans, the same year my husband passed away. And the year Fluid Jiggy had a dove float from his heart, O Lord, the year my mother passed away. I truly loved recalling my life this way, to know that my life mixed with others, not merely based on a mathematical formula calculated on a system of B.C.'s and A.D.'s." Mrs. Hutthutt dried out while talking about the other notable memories she had over time, and Harness put her away, like the others.

Although Harness couldn't completely control how long a person could last out of water, he'd figured most of the "hatching" process out. For example, if it weren't terribly hot, each person took about three days to emerge once they were dropped into the whirlpool of water and lasted anywhere from twelve to fourteen hours out of the water unless, of course, it was raining and the hatched person stayed in the rain. Then they would exist at least as long as the rain did and a few hours after that.

Harness knew that mistakes were part of life, as is sorrow, but still he felt bad that he had lost two people since he'd started hatching the stony eggs—one temporarily and the other for good. During a long and heavy rain storm one night, Gene Rifflebutts had drifted out of the pool of water and into Fargas Union.

Naturally, the loss of Mr. Rifflebutts had been a mistake. Harness had been preparing to start on some carpentry inside the old general store. So, a couple of days earlier, he'd dropped Mr. Rifflebutts into the water. As luck would have it, it was Halloween day when it started to rain real heavily, but Harness didn't really think about the amount of rain falling. He just keep right on working with some floor boarding he was replacing. After it had been raining pretty hard, at least four hours, it crossed Harness' mind that if it rained enough, the water level in the pool might rise and cause the whirlpool to change just enough that it might spit Mr. Rifflebutt out and he'd wash downstream. Strangely, this had never been a concern for Harness before. Harness kind of laughed and thought about the irony of Mr. Rifflebutts coming to life in Fargas Union on Halloween night. Even more ironic was that while Harness was laughing about the possibility, it was happening.

Chapter Twenty-One

Gene Rifflebutts drifted downstream and rolled up on the shore right in the town limits of Fargas Union. He stood up, ready to walk. Of course, he had no idea how lucky he was to have appeared on Halloween night. If it had been any other night of the year, Sheriff Wallup would have spotted Mr. Rifflebutts right away and probably put him in jail for merely being a stranger. Next, Sheriff Wallup would have questioned Mr. Rifflebutts about his whereabouts, and the secret would have come out; Harness' name would have been revealed. Then the rumors that had percolated around town for so long in Fargas Union would have seemed justified. Someone like Don Barnes would have suddenly become right about Harness, and then he would have been asked to explain everything. It wouldn't have taken long before chaos would have broken loose. However, being Halloween, the few kids and parents who saw Mr. Rifflebutts were merely left to wonder who had done such a good job of dressing up.

Just as twilight was running out, Harness went to double check on Mr. Rifflebutts. In a lackadaisical fashion, he glanced in at the whirlpool, positive he would see the emerging form of Gene, but then his adrenalin kicked in. "Oh my, for the love of peat moss, he's really gone!" Harness thought, in disbelief.

The road to Fargas Union followed the river most of the way. Harness looked along the edge of the river the whole way, although, since the sun had gone down, it was pretty futile. His biggest fear was that Mr. Rifflebutts had floated all the way to Fargas Union and was already walking around.

Going slow enough to keep an eye out for Mr. Rifflebutts, the drive to town took a bit over an hour. Recalling that there was a large bend in the river as it entered Fargas Union, Harness decided to start his foot search there. Parking at the bend in the river, leaving his headlights on, Harness stepped out of the truck and saw that there were footprints coming out of the river. He leaned back into the truck, turned off the truck's ignition and began to walk the hundred or so yards toward the first building in Fargas Union.

As he rounded the corner of the building, Harness saw Mr. Rifflebutts. He was about two houses away from where Don Barnes and Georgie Buck Able were sitting waiting for the trick-or-treaters to come up for some candy. Harness, who was now closing in, walking in the shadows, could hear the two men talking about Mr. Rifflebutts as he meandered past them. Don was having a hoot trying to guess who'd dressed up with smooth, slicked black hair and a loose-knit three-piece suit.

"Musta been ol' widow Evelyn Stimbuckle, that's what I'd say. You see that strange sleepy walk? She always was a rock-a-billy music freak, for crying out loud. All's she missing is some smooth suede shoes," said Don Barnes.

"Yippee yes-sir-ee, you're right again, and what a treat-of-a-trick she is. To think, a woman dressed as a man, ha, that done takes the big ol' cakewalk," chimed in Georgie Buck Able.

Once Mr. Rifflebutts had walked beyond the sight of Don Barnes and Georgie Buck Able, Harness caught up to him, motioning him over into the shadows of a big pine tree, whispering, "Gene, Gene, over here, it's Harness." But Gene didn't seem to hear. Harness then ran over and grasped Gene's arm. Gene looked over at Harness slowly. He tried to speak, and that's when

Harness saw that Gene had come ashore too early, before he'd been ready: his ears and mouth had not fully formed yet, and only his nose was allowing him to breath. His arms were shaking as well. Carefully, Harness guided Gene to the truck and drove him home.

*****

Harness had lost another man, Mr. Tullet Bloodsuck. Tullet Bloodsuck had hatched about three times faster than anyone else, and when he hatched, he was so hyper that Harness didn't get to greet him but was stuck watching him run in spastic and crazy circles, away and around, back and forth into the distance. Mr. Bloodsuck was simply a bad joke with a poor punchline. Fading in and out as he weaved back and forth, Harness noticed that Tullet started drying out faster than anyone else.

Tullet Bloodsuck wasn't out of the water half an hour before he'd shrunk halfway. On what ended up being his last run around, Harness saw that Mr. Bloodsuck was turning into pieces. What looked like bits of sand were crumbling off of Mr. Bloodsuck. Before long, he had fallen apart completely. Harness could find nothing of him but chips and flakes lying on the ground. Right before his very eyes, Tullet had disintegrated completely.

Interestingly, Tullet did continue to live in a small way. For the next seven months, whenever it rained steadily, for an hour or so Mr. Bloodsuck's laughter would lightly emit from of the spots where his remains had spread across the ground.

Chapter Twenty-Two

One evening, with the first hints of autumn in the air, a little more than a year after having hatched each person, Harness wondered how he might be able to fully complete the restoration of the town. He now realized that restoration was more than just bringing back some old buildings.

Harness recalled what Mr. Henry Harsh had told him about the Spiral Ring and the manner in which everyone sat and told each other stories. He had been invigorated by Ms. Rubia's talk of the passing of time based on stories and decided that he was going to bring everyone together again. His goal was to plan the event so that it would coincide with a long and steady, slow autumn drizzle.

Harness needed to do a few things to organize. First, he went into Fargas Union to figure out the train schedule. He found that the train came to Fargas Union once a week with freight, on Thursday afternoons. Harness then mailed a letter to the Prohades Zeus Company located in Gunter's Bay, Wisconsin. He'd happened upon the catalog one afternoon after a strong windstorm. It must have blown into town or, then again, maybe Ms. Rubia had placed it where he'd find it. Harness had looked it over. It was a generalized company which offered a wide variety of both practical and specialized gifts and special occasion supplies. Planning the large event, he'd looked it over and written out an order and inserted it into an envelope, along with one of the traveler's checks he still had. Harness had also attached a note to the order, specifying when he'd like the shipment to arrive. He'd consulted the Farmer's Almanac, teamed with his best judgment, to figure out the most likely period for rain in the coming weeks. If all went as scheduled, the rain and the order would arrive at the same time.

The evening before Harness left for town to meet the train, he rolled out a tightly strung fish net which he then spanned across the outside edge of the pool of water. His idea was that when he returned from town with his supplies he was going to try and bring everyone back to life at the same time, which would mean placing everyone in the water at once. The net was a precaution to keep anyone from floating downstream. One experience with that was plenty.

As the day of the event neared, Harness was anxious to get started. He wondered if anyone would talk about turning into parchment so many summers ago. Who would appreciate what had happened as a result of being placed inside jars and bottles during that fateful stretch of sunlight? Would anyone be able to explain how some of them ended up in his mailbox? Would he be allowed to speak; could he ask questions? His mind raced with the possibilities. Wednesday night, as he lay in bed thinking, Harness began to grin. It had started to rain.

Hauling himself inside his truck first thing in the morning, well before his train delivery was due, Harness drove into Fargas Union. He had brought an umbrella and a few slices of bread to eat while he waited. The rain continued to fall, and puddles developed in the potholes on the road. He took his time driving the distance to town. As Harness walked into the train station, he heard Don Barnes and Georgie Buck Able talking. He looked around and saw that they were sitting side by side on one of the benches. He heard Georgie saying, "It's sure something, isn't it Donnie, your daughter coming to town? Guess she'll look a little on the different side after five years, eh?"

"Yep, she's from Boston, you know. She's made a name for herself, just like me here in Fargas. She's a Barnes just the way I taught her to be," Don said.

"She's the ace of clubs, the wild card special, the queen of hearts, a superstar, Donnie. She's a bright and shining superstar!" championed Georgie.

In order to check on the schedule, Harness had no choice but to walk past Don and Georgie. As he came into their view, it didn't take long for them to pipe up.

"Now, now, now, if it's not the man with a thousand rusty nails, a collection of shoddy buildings, a pool of bad water and a pet rock garden to boot. I do declare if you haven't turned out to be well-known stranger around here, Mr. Harness. You're a regular living ghost, a human dustbowl." Harness had kept walking, but then Don added, "Now, hold on a moment there Harness, hold on a minute there."

Harness stopped and looked over.

"A dustbowl, heh heh, good one, Donnie, good one," muttered Georgie Buck Able, who quickly eyed Harness, then looked to the ground, his hands squirming nervously together.

"Waiting for a friend, Mr. Harness?" said Don Barnes with a grin on his face.

"Waiting for the sun to turn to an egg?" added Georgie Buck Able, turning sideways, not looking at Harness at all, but moving his hands together even faster while looking at Don.

"Waiting for a revolution to step off the train?" said Don Barnes.

"Waiting for a revolution, good one, Donnie. I heard they're all out of your size, though, Harness," added Georgie Buck Able, who had started giggling uncontrollably.

"I'm just waiting for the freight, Don. No crime in that, is there?" said Harness.

"Ain't no crime in that, nope, no crime at all." Don answered, a bit stunned, not really expecting that Harness would respond.

"Not a crime, no, sir, not a crime at all," added Georgie Buck Able, still grinning.

"I been wondering, Harness," started Don. "Just who are you? I know most of what goes on around here, but I'll be damned if you don't take the cake away from the icing. Just what's brought you around, and what's been keeping you?"

"The cake off the icing, good one, Donnie," slipped in Georgie Buck Able, now gazing at Harness; however, his smile had disappeared.

Harness had never taken the time to speak with Don or Georgie before, but now he did. "I am the place where I'm living. That's it. I just stopped one day and decided not to move anymore. It's not near as complicated as you're thinking, Don. Just living like you and anyone else would."

At that moment, the train with Don's daughter came chugging around the corner, so both Don and Georgie turned away from Harness, stood up, and walked to the tracks. Don looked back once real quick, and it seemed to Harness as though he gave him a quick nod of approval.

Harness watched Don and his daughter greet each other. They hugged and smiled and began talking. Behind them, Georgie Buck Able was rustling all the luggage together as they all walked out of the train station.

Harness thought that, in some way, he'd wished he could have asked Don about the eggs way back when they'd showed up in his mailbox. Don probably knew more about Fargas Union than anyone. But Harness knew better. If he had mentioned the eggs and the names inside, there's no question, no question at all, how Don would have responded. He would have started some sort of mad and wandering lie: that Harness was messing around with witchcraft, or something as equally suspicious and potentially dangerous.

The rain kept falling. Harness waited, walking around and around the train station, walking outside, picking up old magazines to read and then pacing some more. Eventually he started muttering to himself and pacing back and forth. Phil Slate, the station master, came out and told Harness that the freight train had been delayed five hours. Unfortunately, the five hours eventually turned into a painfully slow three-day wait.

Harness' nerves began to fray. Every once in awhile he'd remember how lucky he was, convincing himself that everything would be okay: the rain would continue, the sun would stay away. He knew that the worst thing he could do was worry and he tried to stop, but he couldn't. He was just too keyed up.

The days of waiting caused him some element of surprise. He was surprised how empty and slow the rail station was. After so much time alone, he had come to think of Fargas Union as representing the busy, hectic city world, yet rarely was there anyone around him. A crowd, he came to realize, was three people. Phil Slate worked the office, and he stuck to himself, much as Harness did. After the first day of waiting, the two of them exchanged periodic glances, a wave, but no conversation. Phil did share the coffee and donuts he brought in each morning; however, the days mostly passed in silence. Harness stayed at the station both night and day. He slept sitting down. The delayed train could come at any moment. The train's official status was "indefinitely delayed."

Mid-afternoon the third day, while staring up at a leak in the roof for the millionth time, Harness heard the whistle of the train from around the last curve leading up to the station. He glanced at Phil Slate, expectant, and Phil nodded his head up and down. "Finally!" Harness said.

When the train came into the station, Harness walked out onto the loading platform, handed his claim tickets to the attendant and gathered up six large boxes, which he carried to the rear of his truck. A small group of people, six in all, not including Phil, were watching him load the boxes, one by one, but, as usual, no one asked him any questions. That was fine, as far as he was concerned. No one would have believed what he had to say, anyway. Plus, he was in a hurry to get home. For some unexplainable reason his luck was holding out. It was still raining and misting, but who knew how long that would last?

CHAPTER TWENTY-THREE

When Harness finally returned to Pick Up Stick City, the first thing he did was double-check the net spanning across the end of the pool of water beneath the waterfall. Then he went ahead as he'd planned. He gathered all the eggs up, all twenty-eight of them, and tossed them into the water at the same time.

He watched as they each sank and tried to fathom how all-encompassing a number as small as twenty-eight had become to him. There, spinning in the water, were twenty-eight lives. "Such a small number," he thought, "but in many ways, they've become my entire life."

Harness then returned to his truck and started unpacking the items he had ordered from the catalog: four big chunks of ice (which he couldn't believe hadn't melted), an ice cream churn, hamburger, onions, pickles, bread, gallons of fresh cream, sugar, vanilla beans, chocolate, balloons, plates, cups and all sorts of necessary supplies to have a festive gathering. Harness busily prepared for everyone's arrival. Based on prior experience, he knew he had about three days to get ready. The rain was still coming down in a wonderfully slow and steady drizzle, and Harness was whistling and singing in pure jubilation.

Harness went to the shore of the pool and greeted each person as they emerged from the water. In about thirty- to forty-minute increments, everyone came to life. There was no need to walk anywhere, no need to stage an event to bring forth excitement, because each person climbed out of the water fully satisfied to recognize each other. Chatter and hugs went around, and Harness felt proud of himself for putting this all together, for understanding the urges and subtle calls for help since he first came to this small, some might say ramshackle collection of ruins. It had been decades since all these people had been together.

Mr. Morgan Bullwhip was the first to emerge. He greeted Harness and was drying off when out came Flench Walk. Immediately the two men hugged, laughed, looked at each other, swore in jubilation, laughed some more and talked about what they had done to help Harness restore the buildings around town. The energy continued as all twenty-eight people climbed out of the water. The last person out, Flannery Hutthutt, joked with everyone, "Okay, so some people walk on water, others try to cross over to the other side of the river, but not us. We just walk through water, right back where we came from."

After everyone had come to the shore, Harness invited them to the center of the old town. There he had laid out all the ingredients for the party. For a moment no one could really believe what they were seeing, but soon everyone was sharing stories with one another, sitting around eating ice cream and hamburgers just as they used to. Watching his new friends, Harness understood he had waited a long time for this day to arrive and more than anything wanted to just observe and enjoy. He also knew that he didn't have to tell all these people that he loved them. That had been taken care of in the making of the vanilla ice cream.

After a while he led a tour around the old town, showing everyone what he had been up to since his arrival and explaining what he was hoping to do over the next few years.

The drizzle switched to a light but steady mist, and what little wind there had been faded away and stillness took over. Everyone had more or less talked the jitters out their systems and, for whatever reason, quit talking and seemed content just to be together. Then, more out of impulse and reflex, really, everyone began drifting back toward the edge of the river to a large grassy area that several people had pointed out to Harness in prior conversations. This was where the Spiral Ring tradition was held.

The townsfolk arranged themselves, one beside the other, out into a small spiral. No one said a word. They just sat and held hands. Finally, somebody spoke.

"I want like to talk about something I remember." Harness looked over and was surprised to see that it was Mr. Reuben Stalkgrunt who had spoken, his lower lip quivering just slightly.

When Harness had first hatched Mr. Stalkgrunt, he hadn't said a thing. Nothing. He'd just sat. He'd wheezed and gawked at the buildings being rebuilt by Harness and seemed to be somewhere between awkward and embarrassed. It was obvious he didn't like being looked at and seemed ashamed of himself, as though his life had been a failure to have ended up in a pool of water. The only thing he'd said that time was that he wished to be returned and left to sleep inside his rock under the water again. And Harness had promised that.

So when Harness heard Mr. Stalkgrunt start speaking, he was startled. Mr. Stalkgrunt was made of few words but for some reason thought this moment was the moment to speak.

"I was declared a worker by my grandfather when I could only hear and not yet talk. I was able to craft together birdhouses when I was only three years old, I was told. My uncle on my mother's side taught me handicrafts when the other grownups were away at parties. He also showed me other skills, such as how to locate water with sticks. I've been fluent in using a divining rod ever since. I never joined any clubs to take care of the natural world, none of them wilderness groups for me, but I bet I saved more trees than all of them put together. I planted thousands and thousands of seedlings every year. I never had time for being social. I just cared about the world and the earth.

"I never wanted to be an engineer, or a chemist, or a biologist. Sure, I had the skills, folks would say, but it wasn't a social title I wanted. Plus, when I was little, I could barely read, had to have vowel lessons, and never could pass a test of any kind that involved reading and holding a pen or a pencil at the same time. This, teamed with the fact that I couldn't imagine not having cuts all over my hands, made it inevitable that I would mostly live in sheds surrounded by hand tools.

"See, all I wanted was to be a woodworker, to make barns, to grow plants, and fish for trout. I just wanted to be outside alone, walking the land, looking for mushrooms or berries, paying attention to birds and weather, sunsets, sunrises and the passing of the seasons. I wanted to belong to long hours of toil and the sawdust of wood. I declared my boundaries early on, and my mother, who worshipped the career of my brother in medicine, talked in anguish and disappointment behind my back. She told others it was only a matter of time before I settled down and became something real and respectable. Everyone would chime in, 'All this fooling around with wood and mushrooms will get him nowhere, don't you know. He has thought about the university, hasn't he?' they'd ask my mother.

"What people couldn't, wouldn't, didn't want to understand was that I was meeting my expectations head on, hammering and nailing my wishes together. One day I realized that I wasn't fit for society and left for good, tucking a wishbone in my back pocket to use when I reached my first crossroads. And when I did come to it,

I yanked the wishbone in half and went in the direction of the big half. My plan was to go the way of my wishes, and after a week, maybe a month of walking, I would use a divining rod to help find a source of water and then stop moving for good.

"I did find a good trail and a good source of water, right where we are now. I became an alchemist and learned to speak with fire, water, earth and air, plus, I'll admit it, I worked with spirits, too. If you look at me right now, you'll see that dreams can come true."

He paused and slowly looked around at everyone in the spiral. "At first it was just myself and Decker Tab's grandfather, Stern Tab," he continued. "We met here because of the waterfall. We had followed different trails, but we had a lot in common. We were each making up our own lives the way we wanted to. Being social was not something we shared, and we were glad to just go about our business. We waved to each other and communicated with our saws and hammers. From time to time we'd talk, and this ended up being better than either one of us expected. There was a period of time when we worked and made all we wanted on our own. We were both content then. One day, though, Stern came up with the idea to make a bank and a general store. He decided that we should provide a good place for others to live, an actual town. I wish I had kept that wishbone I'd carried with me earlier. Fate was teetering right then. I could feel it. I was afraid that inviting people to join us was exactly the wrong thing to do. Stern believed, on the other hand, that if we made a town according to what the two of us believed in, we would enjoy the people who arrived. We solved our problem as I had earlier in life. We pulled a wishbone we'd kept from a recent dinner, and Stern got the big half. I agreed to help him construct the town. I was pretty sure it was a mistake, but a deal's a deal. Living by your word is the building block of honesty.

"We put our skills together and went about the act of creation. The two of us both loved to build, and so we worked with a kind of zest that was blinding. Then along came a stranger and another and another, and they would each stay, filling in the houses we had made, and then ask to work at the stores and bank we had provided. Then along came a rather ravishing young lady, and, before long, she had moved in with Stern. Then they got married, with me as witness and make-shift pastor. Shortly thereafter Decker's father, Flabber Tab, was born, our first native.

"It wasn't done out of spite, but after Stern married, I just decided to move to the edge of town. More and more people started coming to our town. We had seventy-five, maybe eighty at one point, and I just wasn't comfortable. I knew making homes and offering jobs was a mistake. Stern turned out to be more capable of social aspects than I was. He took a liking to community planning and social events.

"Stern wanted to be a success with people more than he was any good at it, though. He was much too polite to organize and far too honest for his own good. He believed whatever people said and, as a result, got pushed around and eventually lost control of the town. Although he could utilize everything a cord of wood had to offer, he lost this sense of economy when he tried working with people. Stern died with hands so white and smooth that unless you had known him years earlier, you would have thought he never knew what a hammer looked like. He'd become so wrapped up in meetings and laws and other people's lives that, in my opinion, he forgot who he really wanted to be.

"It was not until Stern's grandson, Decker, came along that a member of the Tab family finally showed some promise at being able to deal with other people. Unfortunately, just like his grandfather Stern, Decker went one step too far in his social skills. He started making people mad. He went the opposite way of Stern. He ended up not trusting anyone or anything. He thought he had the right to decide what people would and could do. He forgot to offer choices. He wanted to be the center of attention and in charge of everyone forever.

"Decker wasn't able to grow up, plain and simple. He could motivate, but he couldn't produce. He wasn't able to stand by what he said. He was a master of the short-term memory, though. For some unexplainable reason, people would always like him when the elections came around.

"Then he got worse. He got the worst sickness of all. Decker began to believe he deserved to live in a perfect world. It was a joke to me. I would watch Decker and shake my head—the way he lived, thinking that he ought to have his meals cooked and served on silver platters, that he ought to get what he wanted when he wanted it.

"Things quit working right. Even my dog took to doing his business on the cornerstone of Decker's office every morning, which was no small indication of things to come; this was a four-mile trot each way. Next, crows started hovering and flying over his head wherever he went, landing and making a murder of themselves each evening. This was, for me, a sign that the town was on the way out.

"As far as I was concerned, the very inspiration the town was built upon had burned out. The sun coming was inevitable. The place was burning up anyway, so what difference did it make? I watched as the town fell apart. Mold and dry rot took over. No one cared anymore. They would just move away or paint over rust. As things got worse, people divided up into more and more committees and held more and more meetings until finally no one agreed with anyone.

"I knew the place was bound to destroy itself even earlier, though. There were plenty of signs. The strange agribusiness man, the one who tried to kick me off my land, was growing crops, grain he called it, that he fortified with drugs, not with elements of the earth. I later found out that he was offered government subsidies if his grain practices ever failed. Well, since he was farming like a fool, it was pretty obvious he'd be getting government money before too long. One day I thought I'd go have a talk with him, but it turned out he lived about six hundred miles away and was using a phone to farm with.

"The water that we were all supposed to drink was getting thick and chewy with slime and saturated with all kinds of chemicals and gunk. The hops we were famous for turned sour, the turtles got two heads, and the trout couldn't breath. The once-clear river had thick layers of rootbeer-like foam all over it, and in-between the foam were oil slicks reflecting rainbows in the sun. The river flowed by and told me everything I needed to know. Of course, by this time, when I told people the troubles coming up, I was just laughed at. I was so old, people just chuckled when I spoke. Instead of being treated as an elder with vision and wisdom, I was seen as old-fashioned, irrational, senile, half-cracked.

"When the sun did take over, and Decker had finally dried up, it was all I could do from being the first person to jump in the water with a rock tied to my ankles. I had seen all I wanted to see of this place."

Mr. Stalkgrunt stopped talking and let out a slow hissing breath. He looked exhausted and frustrated, sad yet heroic, all at the same time.

He started to speak again, barely able to keep his head up. "I can tell that many of you are surprised to find out who I am. If you're thinking I must be pretty old, you're darn right I am. Well over three generations now."

Mr. Stalkgrunt swallowed hard, took another breath and rested a moment. Then, with a loud clearing of his throat, he revved up his voice again. "Well, the last thing I built was right before I jumped in the water to escape the hot, shadow-splitting sunshine. I stuck a little bit of sand in my mouth, right up against my gum and bottom lip. I felt I was destined to be a dead man anyway, so I thought I'd die with hope in my mouth. I never thought it'd work, but when Harness brought me back out of the water, just like he did with all of you, I found a pearl against my lip. See here, a big white pearl."

Mr. Stalkgrunt reached in his mouth and pulled out a brilliant pearl. He passed the glimmering pearl around the circle, and while it was being shared and admired, Harness noticed the rain had stopped falling and that everyone was beginning to fade away.

By the time the pearl had been passed around and ended back up in Mr. Stalkgrunt's hand, everyone in the spiral was well on his or her way to becoming small white stony eggs again. Even Mr. Stalkgrunt. When his pearl ended up back in his hand, he looked at Harness, nodded his head, placed the pearl back in his mouth and then crumbled up into a mound of dry sand. Right there on the spot.

Harness sat alone, silent for a time, thinking about what Reuben had said, when he noticed that the pearl was lying atop the pile of sand which had once been Mr. Stalkgrunt. Harness picked the small shiny pearl up, held it in his hand and admired the smooth and reflective surface. It was the last creation of a man dedicated to building his dreams and who, much like himself, had created a place on earth.

Without even thinking about it, Harness stuck the pearl in his mouth.

He could taste it. It was the simple flavor of clean water, not spectacular as he thought it might be. Harness let the pearl roll around inside his mouth, and while he did, he heard a voice urging him to listen closely. Straining to hear, Harness sat without moving. He even stopped his breath to listen to the voice. Slowly he made out the words: "The center of the world, you've found the center of the world."

Yes, this had been his quest so many years ago, to find and live and believe so much in where he lived that he might call his home the center of the world. He marvelled at this stroke of good fortune. Pick Up Stick City was at once his life, his memory, his source of story and sorrows, a true and unwavering center.

Harness also understood that someday he would be just like Mr. Stalkgrunt—tired and worn out with life—and, at some point, he wouldn't need his body anymore. He would then pass this pearl along to someone else. Someday he, too, would be able to say good-bye while at the same time saying hello.

Harness leaned over and gingerly touched the small pile of sand which had once been Mr. Stalkgrunt. He licked his fingertips. The flavor was empty—neither salty nor sweet. The sand would soon blow apart and what remained of Mr. Stalkgrunt would be returned to the earth.

Harness stood up, took a step forward to begin this new phase of his life, but he didn't walk straight. Instead, he began to spin around and around, outward in ever-growing loops, making his own Spiral Ring. What was the question he wanted to ask? Winding his spinning down, he slowly came to a stop and, regaining his balance, noticed that once again, just as when he first arrived in the town, he was being joined by hundreds of birds, all hovering, landing beside him, joining him as he rejoiced in the miracle of this small, tiny little place in the universe. He even thought he heard a duck call going off somewhere.

As far as Harness was concerned, he was standing directly in the middle of the world: in the middle of time, in the middle of space. Raising his arms straight above his head, he shouted thanks to the world and the birds scattered upward, whirled around him in a flurry of shadowed flight, finally twisting and splitting into glints of rainbowed light.

Steve Semken lives in North Liberty, Iowa and has authored mostly nonfiction essays dealing with ties between spirituality and the natural world. His most recent book, *The Great Blues (Woodley Press, Washburn Univ., Topeka, Kansas, 2005)* is a creative, nonfiction exploration into the habits and habitat of the great blue heron. *Pick Up Stick City* is his first long work of fiction. Steve has run the Ice Cube Press since 1993 and has been Director of the Standing By Words Center since 1998.